"*Justine* has the perfect electric feeling of that crush you have on the person you want to be next, when you don't know any better, and you can't tell if you're running away from them or toward them. Harmon's mix of text and image is seamless, intimate, a continuous dream, and *Justine* brings her talents together with formidable force and grace. A showstopping debut."

—**ALEXANDER CHEE**, author of *How to Write an Autobiographical Novel*

"I've known Forsyth Harmon by the luxurious, eerie lines of her illustrations for years, and what a joy to discover that her writing is just as rich as her drawings. *Justine* beautifully captures the ragged-edged complexities of female friendship and the raw force with which a teenage girl moves through the turbulence of her previously quiet life. *Justine* functions like an illuminated manuscript, in which illustration can live independently yet brings wealths of new meaning to a text, weaving together a world that's pulsingly alive."

—**KRISTEN RADTKE**, author of *Imagine Wanting Only This*

"Forsyth Harmon tells powerful stories in both word and image, the two working together to convey meaning and emotion in a way that's deeply satisfying. As a writer, and an artist, her gifts are on full display here. *Justine* is unsettling, adoring, insightful, and even a little frightening. The best books carry insights that will shake you. That's what happened to me in this piercing novel. It shook me, and it made me see."

—**VICTOR LAVALLE**, author of *The Changeling*

"Desire and self-destruction have a way of eclipsing and re-eclipsing each other in adolescence, as we look for reasons to live and ways to avoid living. With nervy, exacting illustrations and effortless prose, Forsyth Harmon's *Justine* chronicles that struggle with the clarity and mystery of a black opal."

—**CATHERINE LACEY**, author of *Pew*

"With reservoirs of emotional intelligence plus pinpoint precision of prose and line, Harmon conjures the world with a vividness peculiar to adolescence: she is devastatingly attuned to something as tiny as the poem of an unspooling cassette, as well as the enormity of those subtle yet life-shifting currents of longing, loathing, and eroticism that can run between two teenage girls. An exquisite book."

—**HERMIONE HOBY**, author of *Neon in Daylight*

"*Justine* is a lushly rendered portrait of suburban teen girlhood in whose urgent and exquisite pages adolescent malaise, disordered eating, and the erotics of obsession are given the gravity of Greek drama. Forsyth Harmon is an artist who understands the holy power of longing."

—**MELISSA FEBOS**, author of *Girlhood*

JUSTINE

Published by Tin House, Portland, Oregon

Distributed by W. W. Norton & Company

Library of Congress Cataloging-in-Publication Data

Names: Harmon, Forsyth, 1979- author, illustrator.
Title: Justine : a novel / Forsyth Harmon.
Description: Portland, Oregon : Tin House, [2021]
Identifiers: LCCN 2020040348 | ISBN 9781951142339 (hardcover) | ISBN 9781951142346 (ebook)
Subjects: CYAC: Friendship--Fiction. | Coming of age--Fiction.
Classification: LCC PZ7.1.H3717 Ju 2021 | DDC [Fic]--dc23
LC record available at https://lccn.loc.gov/2020040348

First US Edition 2021
Printed in the USA
Cover and interior illustrations by Forsyth Harmon
Cover and interior design by Diane Chonette
www.tinhouse.com

Justine

a novel

FORSYTH HARMON

 TIN HOUSE / Portland, Oregon

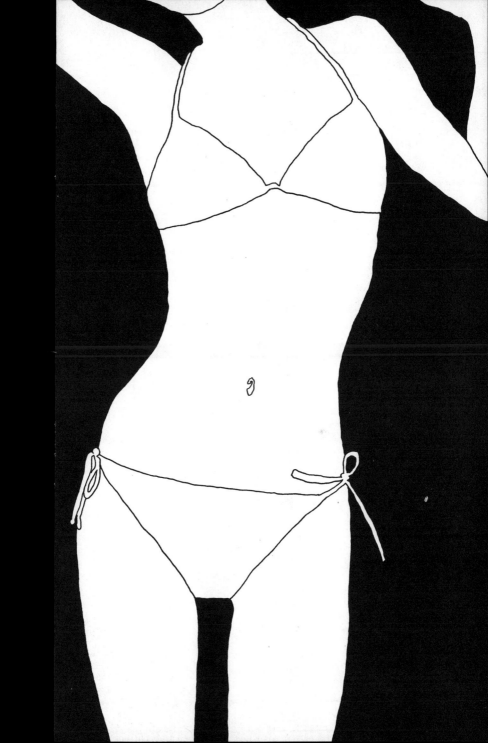

For my mother and her mother—

ONE

I first saw her on the other side of the conveyor belt. She was so tall and thin she looked almost two-dimensional, her long fingers fluttering over the cash register keys, her long arms passing my Trident sugar-free gum and Diet Coke over the sensor. Her own can of Diet Coke sweated a ring on the countertop beside her. Her face was long too, and her skin was so pale it was bluish like skim milk, and transparent in places, veins visible at the temples. Her complexion created an unsettling contrast with her hair, which was cut into a chin-length pitch-black bob. She pulled at the ends of it with those long white fingers, shoving the hair into her mouth, wide and protruding as though closed around the rind of an orange slice. But her eyebrows were so light they were almost nonexistent, and I could see then that her inch-long roots were an ashy color, dull as dishwater. Most girls would've highlighted hair that color, made it blonder. But Justine went dark. There was something spooky about the lighter roots. There was something spooky about Justine altogether. That's what the name tag attached to her red Stop & Shop apron said: "Justine." She must've gone to the other high school, the nicer one the next town over.

1

"Two dollars." Justine looked at me and smiled a wide, bright, dazzling smile. It was like the whole supermarket went silent when she smiled: there was a pause in the fitful beeps of scanned barcodes; the tinny music faded away. Her smile lit me up and exposed me all at once. Justine was the light shining on me and the dark shadow it cast, and I wanted to stand there forever in the relief of that contrast.

I handed her the money, and when the tips of my fingers brushed the soft inside of her wrist, my body went hot. It was a heat I didn't feel when I was with Matt. I felt it from the inside, it overwhelmed me, I tried not to show it. I grabbed my gum and soda.

Posters covered the windows—"Sprite Lemon-Lime Soda, 12-pack, $3.49"; "Boboli Original Pizza Crust, 2 for $5.00"— admitting natural light in only a few narrow slices. I saw a Help Wanted flyer not far from the automatic doors, just above the gumball machines.

A woman with long hair parted down the middle was stationed at customer service. From afar, I wasn't sure what it was about her that scared me, but as I got closer I realized it was her face, how hairless and smooth it was, deleting any indication of age. She could've been thirty or fifty, and for some reason that frightened me. Her name tag said "Theresa."

"I'm here about the job?" I had to look up at her. The kiosk was raised, giving her a queenly altitude. She was counting postage stamps, mouthing "ten, eleven" with maroon-lined lips. She didn't acknowledge having heard me at first, finally raising her brows, which were entirely penciled in—I don't think there was a single actual hair—and handed down a piece of paper and a pen from her little window with a sigh, like I was really putting her out. The counter was too high to use as a writing surface; I had to use a Tide box at the top of a pyramid-shaped detergent display. I suspected she liked that, seeing me slightly compromised.

I scribbled down my information and handed the form back up to her. She snatched it with a French-manicured hand, and I saw beneath her three-quarter sleeves that her arms were hairless too. Luminescent. She cradled a receiver between her shoulder and ear.

"Michelle to customer service." Her voice sounded nasal over the intercom, more South Shore Long Island than North. She examined the application, looking from it to me, then back at it again, with a seriousness that felt disproportionate to the job.

"Fine." Theresa glared, snapping the paper into a three-ring binder.

And so I secured a place for myself in Justine's glittering vicinity.

*

At home, Grandma was asleep on the couch, knitting needles Xed across her chest, a ball of olive-green yarn on the floor, Fox News on the TV. I dropped my bag and slumped into the La-Z-Boy. Marlena leapt onto my lap and kneaded her claws through my cutoffs, into my thigh. I wrapped my fingers around her neck and pressed my lips to her head.

"You're my best friend," I whispered into her little skull.

She wriggled out of my lock and kept kneading. The light made her pupils into slits. I opened the can of Diet Coke with a crack.

Grandma stirred. "I wasn't sleeping." She shook her head, sitting up and setting her knitting needles on the coffee table, aligning them parallel to the edge. "I was up at 5:00 a.m. this morning scrubbing the kitchen floor." She put on her glasses. "Look at that hair," she said, pointing at the newscaster. "It looks like a chicken scratched in it." I nodded. She repositioned a doily.

"You should've seen *Days of Our Lives* today," she continued, collecting the ball of yarn from the floor. "Hope hypnotized John. And now she's pregnant. She's big as a house."

Marlena stuck out her chin, I stroked her neck. Grandma smiled at me. "How beautiful you look," she said. "My little beauty." She uncapped the tube of Aspercreme she kept on the side table and rubbed the salve into her knuckles. "Matt called."

I leaned back into the chair, popping the footrest. Junior prom was the next day. Marlena settled on my legs. The oscillating fan in the corner made a rattling sound. Grandma switched on the table lamp.

"Horror God," she gasped, pointing at the TV. "The children are shooting? It's come doom-a-day. Are you hungry?"

She opened the coffee table drawer and pulled out a Twix bar. I shook my head. She shrugged and put it back in the drawer, got up, and pulled the lace from the window. She wore her short hair in stiff finger waves, and the back was flat from her nap. "Look how long Vinny's grass is. *Vilken sophög*. It looks like a shithouse. I'm going out to mow our lawn." She petted Marlena's head. "He's so lazy."

"She."

"She, she." Grandma dismissed the cat with a wave. "She doesn't do nothing."

Grandma tied on her orthopedic shoes and put on lipstick. The screen door banged shut behind her. The lawn mower started. I swatted Marlena off my lap. She shot down the hall into my room, and I followed her and closed the door behind us for the night. As I lowered the blinds, I saw it was drizzling. Grandma was mowing the lawn in a shower cap. I slid the scale out from under my bed and tapped it with my toe, waiting for the green zero to appear. One hundred twenty-five pounds still.

*

The next day, the only good thing about junior prom was the feeling of eyes on me: Grandma's in the mirror as I curled my hair; Matt's as he slid a white rose corsage onto my wrist; his parents' as I stretched the length of my neck for photos; his best friend's, in the limo, as I wrapped my lips around the mouth of a vodka bottle.

But later, in a motel room in Hampton Bays, I didn't like the feeling of Matt's eyes on me at all. He saw my body, but that was all he saw. No, Matt didn't even know me. And the next morning, as his truck turned into the driveway to drop me home, I told him it was over.

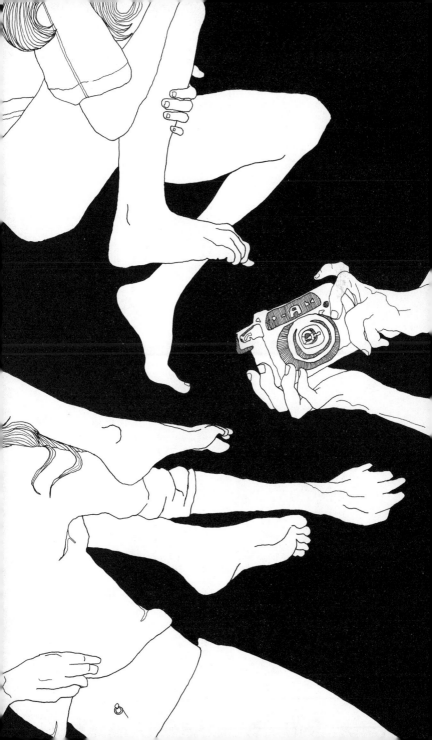

TWO

When Justine lowered the red Stop & Shop apron over my head, it felt like an anointment. A name tag had already been affixed to the left breast. It said "Alison."

"But my name is Ali."

"That's just a nickname." She tugged at my hair.

"It's what my birth certificate says."

"Alison's better." She wrapped the apron strings around my waist and tied them into a neat bow just above my belly button. I flushed with the intimacy of it.

Justine taught me how to bag groceries—how to construct the most efficient bottom-heavy grids, like playing Tetris; how to distribute the weight evenly across each bag; how to bag by category: refrigerated items in one, household cleaners in another. She taught me all the apple PLU codes: Braeburn, 4103; Gala, 4133; McIntosh, 4152. She taught me how to tell the difference between cucumbers (cold, waxy, and bumpy) and zucchini (rough and dry), without once insinuating male genitalia. She showed me how to casually turn my back on a not even very rude customer and spit on her strawberries.

Watching Justine at the register from my end of the conveyor belt, I was learning other things too, things she didn't say—like after I saw her make several trips to the bathroom, I

11

learned that vomiting was one way to counteract eating freely from the candy rack. When she passed items down to me to be bagged, I saw the small red teeth cut-marks on her first and third knuckles.

I learned, during downtimes, which magazines I should and shouldn't read when she actually took away my *Seventeen*, putting it back on the rack and replacing it with *Vogue*. On the cover, Kate Moss's face stood in for the *G*. She was laughing so hard her eyes were closed, her terrible but somehow endearing teeth exposed. She wore nothing but dark denim jeans, her fingers covering her nipples. The thinnest women never look slutty, no matter how slutty they are.

Justine stabbed a finger at Kate's bare stomach. "They say she had ribs removed to accentuate her waist."

"Really?"

Kate was entirely naked on page 185: a tiny square of pubic hair, her nipples erect. How long her nipples were! I brought the magazine to my face. On the next page, in profile, they were grotesque, the left one a little inverted.

"She's only five foot six, you know," Justine said.

"I'm five foot six."

Justine shrugged.

At the end of our shift, Justine offered me a ride. I followed her out back to her old brick-red LeSabre, like that was what we did every day. The interior was immaculate. She pulled down the sun visor and studied herself in the vanity mirror, then fumbled through her purse for a tweezer,

32446

WEED	10	00
SHROOMS	1 0 0	00
ECSTASY	20	00
COKE	5 0	00

HESS
EXPRESS

which she took to her eyebrows with great ferocity, creating little pink wounds where she attempted to prematurely excavate ingrown hairs as though they were mites infesting her brow bone.

When she turned the ignition key, a strange meandering falsetto pealed through the car. I didn't know what the music was, but tapped my fingers on the door handle as though it were familiar. The lyrics posed an existential question about the mind-body divide. Justine sang along. She was so off-key she must've been tone deaf. She didn't put on her seat belt. She took the speed bumps hard and fast, racing toward the adjacent lot, turning into the Hess station. Her bare thighs did not spread across the seat like mine did. They were no wider than her calves. I went up on the balls of my feet to bring mine in a little.

A tall, tan, dark-haired boy shuffled out of the Express Mart, jeans slung low, pant legs so wide you couldn't see his shoes. His Yankees cap sat high on his head, the brim angled forty-five degrees to the side. Justine pulled up to the pump and the boy shook his head. She rolled down the window.

"Tank's on the other side," he said, laughing, flagging us right.

Justine huffed, backed up, and pulled forward to the pump at the other side of the aisle. I rolled down the passenger window and the boy looked in past me at Justine very seriously, dark eyes half-closed, lashes interminable. His nose was large and irregular—he must've broken it—but that one imperfection only seemed to exaggerate his beauty. His name tag said

14

what I thought was "Chris"—I couldn't quite make out the bubbly Sharpie graffiti.

Sitting there between them, I felt ordinary. My thighs spread miserably, my legs were disproportionately short—especially my calves—my torso too long, and my features were too large to be considered fine. My hair was long and thick but coarse—it had the tendency to get frizzy—and my fingers should've been thinner, but my skin was too thin, making me prone to cuts and scars.

Justine stared straight ahead and made her mouth a long straight line. Chris unscrewed the gas cap, filled the tank. Another boy appeared at the driver's side. He pushed himself through the open window, leaned across Justine, and turned off the car stereo. She swatted his wiry arm and opened her mouth around it like she might bite. She had big teeth.

This boy was ugly, with a smug smile and crooked incisors, his freckled features crowded into the middle of his broad white  face, pinched into an expression of demanding dissatisfaction. He looked directly at me with narrow eyes so black I couldn't see into them: it was the look of a person who's heard a rumor about you but won't

say what it is, doesn't care if it's true, actually prefers and even enjoys being offended by you. His name tag said "Ryan."

"Yo," he droned, leaning his forearms against Justine's sill, nodding at me, "who's she?" His fingernails were long, dirt collected beneath them.

Justine reached her arm around me and squeezed. "Isn't she cute?" She kissed me on the cheek and I felt it everywhere. "Alison." I just let her call me that. That's who I would be with these people.

Ryan lifted his chin a little, judging me. His freckles shifted with his expression, and I could tell he disapproved. Yes, he hated me, and I hated myself, which created an unexpected point of agreement between us.

He shoved his hands into his pockets and headed over to the other island, where a van waited. Chris banged on the LeSabre hood twice. Justine switched on the stereo and pulled ahead; she seemed to be leaving without paying. She veered toward Ryan like she might run him over, slammed on the brakes just short of him, then sped out of the lot like none of it had happened.

"That's my boyfriend," she said.

"Which one?"

"What?" she shrieked, turning left without looking right. "You think I'd go out with Ryan?" The person driving the car behind us leaned on the horn hard. "Disgusting." She banged a fist against the steering wheel, laughing. "How could you even think that? No. Christopher."

16

Of course. And yet I couldn't imagine Justine and Chris having sex. I guess I couldn't imagine Justine having sex with anyone. But I could imagine Ryan having sex with pretty much anyone, including me.

Justine drove with just two long fingers touching the wheel. Her other arm was out the window, hand weaving in the wind, wrist arching over and under Country Hot Bagels, Napper Tandy's, Nina's Pizza. She took wide looping turns, entirely unaware of the shoulder, the yellow double line; she sped and slowed erratically as she dipped in and out of one thought or another; she ignored stop signs and slammed on the brakes at the last possible second at the traffic light, causing me to shout; she laughed at me. I gripped the passenger door handle, scared but kind of happily distracted. She sang at the top of her lungs, snaking her head back and forth with the beat, occasionally turning to me, totally unselfconscious, beaming.

I directed her to my street, and she made a wide turn into our driveway.

"Watch the cat!" I pounded the dash.

Marlena bolted across the pebbles into the lilies of the valley.

Grandma was up on the ladder with the hacksaw, cutting off a sugar maple branch. She shouldn't have been doing that. She wiped

17

her forehead, waved the saw at us. She climbed down as I got out of the car.

"That's not Matt." Grandma examined Justine through the windshield. "Matt called."

"I'm Alison's new boyfriend." Justine looked up at Grandma, pulling the ends of her hair into her wide, smiling mouth.

Grandma laughed and waved a hand. "Well of course." Grandma was always pretending she knew what people were talking about. Sweat stained the underarms of her housedress. "What a pretty lady," Grandma said as Justine got out of the car, "and not too fat."

"Grandma!"

"*Vad*? She can't understand what I'm saying," Grandma muttered. "My English is no good."

Justine crouched by the lilies of the valley. "What's your kitty's name?"

"Marlena," Grandma said, "from *Days*."

"*Of Our Lives*," I sighed.

"Austin found Carrie in bed with Michael today." Grandma shook her head, holding the door open for us. Justine sped through the kitchen and poked her head into my room. When she bounced onto my twin bed I wondered why I hadn't taken down that old Mariah Carey poster. I turned a framed picture of Matt and me facedown.

"You have the same sheets as Fiona Apple in the 'Criminal' video," she said.

"I know." I sat on the floor and pinched the flesh at the inside of my thigh.

Justine rolled to her side, propped her head in one hand, and put the other on her hip. She extended her lower leg and crossed her top leg over it, resting her foot on the bed. She should've taken her shoes off. She breathed deeply and deliberately, lifting her bottom leg on exhale, lowering it on inhale. "Do this," she said, repeating the motion.

I mirrored her.

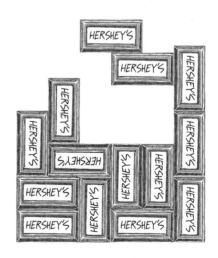

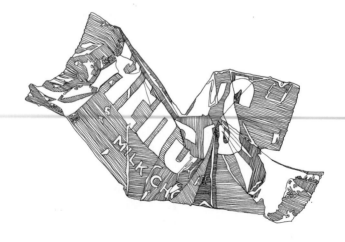

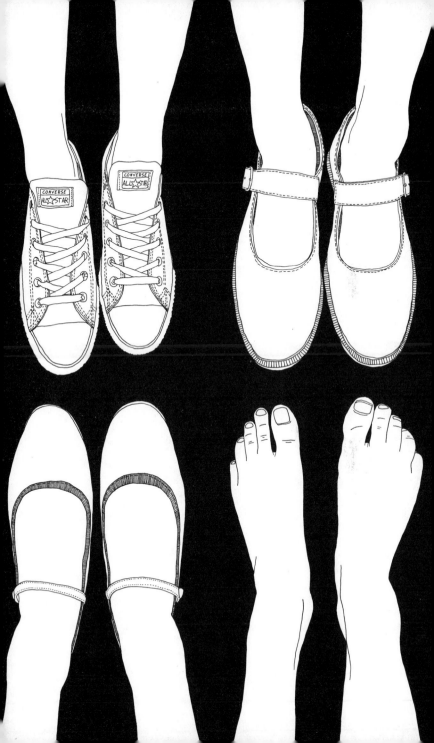

THREE

The Walt Whitman Mall's exterior walls were engraved with poetry. It looked like a huge tomb. I followed Justine through heavy glass doors, out of the wet heat. The concourse was dark and depressing and smelled like pretzels. In the Victoria's Secret display, a girl in a floral-embroidered peach silk bra and panties stood at a window, fingers resting on the sill, looking out intently. The room glowed warm and blurry behind her, pink satin sheets shimmering. In the Ralph Lauren display, a girl carried a soccer ball across a deep-green sports field in orange heels, long blonde ponytail flagging after her. Two bare-chested boys flanked the Abercrombie entrance. They sprayed cologne at us.

The Bloomingdale's beauty department was cool, bright, and gleaming, with shiny black-and-white-checkered floors and gorgeous grids of every color eye shadow: metallic blacks, oranges, and greens like butterfly wings; silvers and opals like something from outer space; flat chemical pastels like conversation hearts: call me, kiss me, love me. A woman worried over a small, round, lit-up mirror, blending a different shade of olive concealer into either cheek, checking one side of her face, then turning her head to compare it with the other.

Justine picked up a bottle of Polo Sport. "Did you know," she asked, nodding at the model's face on the perfume display, "Bridget Hall only has an eighth-grade education and a weakness for red meat?"

Bridget looked as though she'd just reached the mountaintop after a long hike, almost perspiring, shrugging off a sweatshirt to reveal a tight tank top underneath, the letters "USA" stretched across her chest. Justine dropped a set of keys to the floor, then bent down to pick them up and slipped a bottle of Clinique Happy into her bag. My chest got tight. I hadn't expected that. I looked around at saleswomen behind the counters, cameras affixed to the ceiling. Justine shook her head and linked her arm with mine. I watched our feet cross the black-and-white-checkered tile, matching my step to hers. It made me feel like I was with her—like I almost was her—like I was free to enjoy the thrills of her exploits while being exempt from their consequences. We rode the escalator up arm in arm. I tried to slow my breath, my heart.

Justine browsed swimsuit racks with brisk efficiency, occasionally pausing to look at something more closely. When she found something she liked, she handed me the hanger. Soon I had a whole armful.

"Ten items," she told the fitting room attendant, waving me

26

into the little room after her. I sat on the stool in the corner and counted eleven hangers. She pulled her dress over her head and dropped it to the floor, naked except for underwear. She didn't need a bra; that's how flat her chest was. I sort of hunched a little, hiding my own. I held my breath as she sorted through the hangers on my lap, settling on a Calvin Klein string bikini. I watched her slip it on in the three-way mirror. I think she liked me watching her like that, maybe even needed me to do it. I stared at the gap between her thighs, my body buzzing. I crossed my legs, popped two pieces of Trident. She peeled a security tag from the bikini bottom and stuck it under my stool, her chest in my face. She held the bikini strings at the nape of her neck.

"Knot them?" she asked, turning toward the mirror again.

I stood, nose even with a trail of fine ashy hairs at her nape, and tied a bow, then patted it lightly, touching her neck. We smiled at each other in the mirror. She put her dress back on over the bikini and we walked out of the fitting room like nothing, giving friendly nods to the attendant, but everything was loud, bright, and weird, like some kind of incandescent version of the mall.

Patent leather shoes shone on a multitiered display like sweets on a tray. Justine grabbed a black Mary Jane and shook it in the salesgirl's face.

"Nine," she demanded.

Our feet were the same size. We sat and waited on a mauve velvet bench. I tucked the bikini strings into her dress. She took her shoes off. So did I. We put our feet side by side. Mine were wider, toenail polish still chipped pink from junior prom. Her toenails were painted black.

The salesgirl brought out a pebbled navy-blue box with "Prada" gold-embossed on the top. Just the box itself was beautiful. Justine removed a shiny black shoe from its white felt bag and slipped her foot inside, buckling the thin strap at her ankle. She raised her leg. We admired it.

Once the salesgirl had disappeared in back, Justine put my sneakers into the empty Prada box and pushed her old lug sole Mary Janes toward me. Her breath was hot in my ear as she whispered: "You wear my shoes."

It felt intimate, sliding my feet inside. We leapt up, me in her shoes and her in the new ones, and left the department store arms linked. Passing back out those heavy glass doors into the humidity, I felt lit up and invincible, like when you catch that bouncing star in *Super Mario*. I felt nothing but my heartbeat.

We drove along Jericho Turnpike, past Jiffy Lube, Petland, Tattoo Lou's. Some Hondas and pickup trucks pulled out of the Saint Francis parking lot, others into the Taco Bell drive-through, arms hanging from windows, cigarettes dangling from fingers.

I drove Justine home. Her street was lined with shabby split-levels, the shingle stain, shutter color, and lawn mainte-nance level varying but the layouts all the same. As we pulled up to her house, it started to rain. The potted plant on the stoop was dead. The metal number 7 on the front door was missing a nail and hung askew in a way that made me sad. Inside, the house was quiet and underlit. There was a woman sitting in the kitchen. I assumed she was Justine's mother, but she didn't look up from her newspaper as we came in.

Justine curled her fingers around the iron banister and started up the stairs. What beautiful calves she had, long and nar-row. Her new black pat-ent leather shoes clacked against each uncarpeted step. I felt like I was following her into a dark trap.

Justine's walls, comforter, and furniture, the phone sitting on the hardwood floor by her bed: everything in her room was white. None of her personal belongings in sight, the room looked medical, sterile—I even smelled rubbing alcohol—with the exception of maybe a hundred magazine pages taped to the wall above the bed. There was a girl sitting in a shopping cart full of bowling balls for Guess, her long, dark, messy curls hanging to her waist. A hunched, eerie little blonde with heavy-lidded eyes posed in a shiny white trench for Jil Sander. Another one with a high forehead did a high kick in heels for Versace. In a Calvin Klein ad, Christy Turlington wriggled into a pair of jeans, a few strands of hair falling across her face.

"Christy Turlington weighs fifteen pounds less now than she did in high school," Justine said.

And then there was that image of Kate Moss in the same string bikini Justine was wearing under her dress.

A notebook sat open on Justine's nightstand. The handwriting was all caps, tiny and neat. It read: "Tuesday: 3 containers Dannon Light fat-free strawberry yogurt: 300; 8 oz.

low-fat ground turkey: 300; 4 oz. Häagen-Dazs raspberry sorbet: 150." And that was it: 750 calories. On the opposite page: a line chart, tracking her weight over several days. I didn't want to look too long. I felt a little sick. I sat down on the bed and the sickness mutated into a kind of nervous arousal. Justine straddled the only other seat in the bare room, a small stationary bicycle in the corner. She tucked her long feet into the stirrups and rested her skinny forearms against the handlebars like a praying mantis.

*

On the way home, I went by the Stop & Shop. The parking lot glistened in the streetlight, slick with rain. Thick mist rose from the asphalt. There were just a few cars, several abandoned shopping carts. The windows gave off a hazy yellow glow. I went inside. The selection of yogurts was extensive in the cool dairy aisle. I found the neat little rows of cups calming, the mixed berry and vanilla bean pictures reassuring. I placed fifteen containers of Dannon Light fat-free strawberry yogurt into my basket.

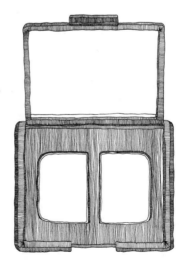

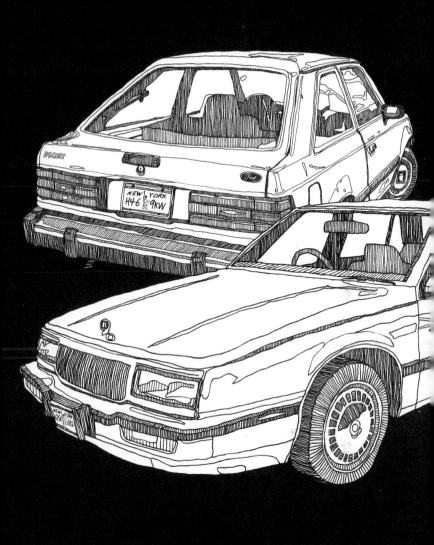

There was only one register open. On the cover of *Rolling Stone*, Britney Spears reclined on hot-pink satin sheets in a black push-up bra and polka-dot boy shorts, holding a stuffed purple Teletubby, telephone receiver to her ear. "The Diana We Never Knew" smiled sheepishly on the cover of *People*. She shrugged, pressing her cheek to her bare shoulder in a way that seemed both humble and arrogant. I didn't understand why people were so obsessed with Princess Diana. Her haircut was so weirdly dated, and she'd been dead for like two years. I put a copy of *Vogue* on the conveyor with the yogurts.

The tag affixed to the checkout girl's red apron read "Michelle." I didn't know her—we hadn't shared a shift yet. She stuck out her thick lower lip and blew thin blonde hair back from her forehead, which was a bit narrower than her puffy jowls, giving her face an egg shape. The key sticking out of her register drawer teemed with key chains—a Tamagotchi, the Eiffel Tower, a mini Koosh, "Miami" in pink script. She passed the yogurts over the sensor with the white billowy hand of a baby, knuckles dimpled. When she punched one brown bag into another, I worried the thick paper would irritate her tender skin.

As I passed the Hess station, I thought I maybe saw Ryan leaning into a red convertible.

*

34

At home, the house was dark except for light from the television flickering from our front window. The neighborhood was quiet except for the pebbles sounding under the tires, the crickets.

"Horror God, that Governor Bush is disgusting," Grandma called from the living room in greeting. "He looks like a—what do they call them?"

I set the grocery bag on the floor and opened the fridge, lighting the kitchen.

"Squirrel!" she shouted. "At least Clinton is good-looking."

I knelt and moved an aluminum foil–wrapped dish up a shelf.

"Have the banana cream pie or it'll go bad."

I lined up the yogurts on the empty shelf.

"You were at Matt's house?" Grandma called over the *Ally McBeal* opening credits. "How's he?"

"We broke up."

"*Nej.* He's so handsome. And Ally, she's so nice. Don't you like Ally? Ali, like you." I heard the candy dish clatter on the coffee table. "*Förbaskade katten!*"

Marlena raced into the kitchen.

"Don't hit her!" I yelled.

"He's *klo*!"

"This isn't a farm," I muttered. "*Jag vet,*" I whispered to the cat, filling her food bowl. I rubbed her sides, feeling her little ribs. Eating was the only time she let me do that.

I rooted around the junk drawer for a bottle of black nail polish and sat down on the couch next to Grandma with my dinner: one strawberry yogurt.

35

Grandma's face crumpled in disgust. "At least take bread with it." She was having a slice of pie.

I took my shoes off and put my feet on the coffee table.

"New shoes?" She frowned at Justine's old lug soles. "From Penney's?"

"There's no *s*." I applied polish to my big toes.

"*Vad*?"

"Penney. J. C. Penney. There's no *s* on the end." The pinkie toes were impossible. They hardly had nails. "Do you know who Walt Whitman is?"

"The mall?"

"The poet."

"*Vem*?"

"The poet!"

"Well of course," she said. She didn't, though.

"He was gay."

"Who was?"

I sighed.

"They sued Jenny Jones."

"Who?" I asked.

"The gays."

Calista Flockhart fluttered across the screen like a little idiot bird in a skirt suit.

"I hate this show."

"You miss *Highway to Heaven*?" Grandma flipped through channels. "I miss *Highway to Heaven*." Piercing horns announced her favorite game show. "*Millionaire*!" she exclaimed, clasping her hands to her chest.

I got in bed and paged through *Vogue*. They'd dressed up a girl with dark hair and wide-set eyes like Queen Amidala. She was frightening in white face paint and red spots penciled on each cheek, head hanging almost as though her neck were broken from the weight of her huge headpiece. On another page, three girls in red lipstick fought over a messenger bag. The girl wearing the bag held her hands up in surrender. Her eyes were covered by a second girl's hands—this girl had snuck up behind her. A third girl with braids held garden shears to the strap, just about to cut. I tore out the page. I meant to tape it to the wall but found myself suddenly tired and even a little dizzy. I put the magazine down and lay back. My body was fizz, frothing, effervescent, a can of just-opened Diet Coke. I was so light it was like I was lifting—levitating—up from the bed, through the roof, over our tiny house, the trees, the school, hovering above all of Huntington—all of Long Island. I was so high nothing could touch me.

I felt the weight of Marlena land on the bed beside me. She stepped in little circles, collapsing into a ball next to my head. I stroked her temples. She purred quizzically. Her tail beat the mattress.

FOUR

They looked like ghosts, the boys, skateboarding across the Stop & Shop back lot at dusk. Justine and I took off our aprons. I walked toward Grandma's car, Justine toward Chris. She stood in his path; he spun his board, leaned back, and skidded to brake inches from her. Ryan slowed to a stop, kicked his board upside down, and climbed into the passenger side of the car just as I got behind the wheel.

Why was he in the car? I felt that same self-consciousness, like he knew something about me I didn't. He pulled a little plastic bag from his shirt pocket and rolled a joint, narrowing those black eyes, carefully tearing and folding the paper, sprinkling weed into the crease.

"This shit"—he lit the joint and took a first puff—"is sinsemilla." He ejected my tape from the stereo without even asking, holding it up in reprimand. It was Mariah Carey's *Butterfly*. He tossed it to the floor, fished a cassette from his pants pocket, and popped it into the deck like he'd been riding shotgun in Grandma's car all his life.

"Mariah Carey went to my high school," I said.

He shrugged, handed me the joint, and exhaled. "Bust a lung."

I took a long drag. "She does have an incredible vocal range."

The music started out like static, like tuning into a radio station.

"Do you know who this is?" he asked. I was pretty sure he knew I didn't know, and the whole point was to see how stupid he could make me feel, sitting there, not knowing.

"It's not a test," he said.

It was a test. The beat kicked in. I shrugged.

"Aesop Rock, 'Wake Up Call,' featuring Percee P, from the '97 album *Music for Earthworms*." He said it in a kind of monotone, looking into the distance as though he were reading, like it was written out there in the trees. "But I guess Mariah Carey's the only local music you know."

"Billy Joel."

"Billy Joel." He looked like he might spit.

"'Only the Good Die Young' is a good song though, no?" I sort of half sang that part about the white confirmation dress, immediately regretting it.

"Aesop Rock went to my high school," he said.

Northport kids always thought they were so cool, just because they had more art classes and drugs. We sat and hotboxed and listened to the rolling hip-hop bass, watching Justine watch Chris skate in the dimming dusk. The streetlights switched on, washing through the car and turning the smoke gold. I couldn't tell if the music was good or not.

"You know what they say about her, right?" I asked.

"Justine?" He blew smoke. "Yeah. She's fucking nuts."

"Mariah Carey. She never went to class, but when she did, she just sat in the back, and when a teacher called on her to like, answer a question—"

He flipped the *Music for Earthworms* tape case in his hands, inspecting the label. "Isn't this album cover dope?"

"—no matter what it was, she'd just shrug and be like, 'I'm gonna be a singer.'"

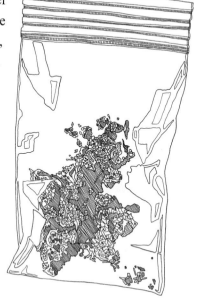

He pulled the insert from the case and unfolded it.

"Isn't that funny?"

Nothing. Just him and the insert.

"They say she beat up all the cheerleaders. And she gave this guy my friend knows a drawing of her body with notes about all the things she wanted him to do to it."

At that he looked over at me with a crooked grin, but was immediately distracted by Chris pitching his arms and twisting his hips with an easy grace, gaining speed, grinding the edge of his skateboard on the curb dividing parking aisles. Chris popped his board into the air, tucking his knees while it flipped 360 degrees, then landed on it neatly and continued rolling without losing speed. What an elegant creature. Ryan got out of the car, like we hadn't even been talking, leaving the door wide open, music spilling out into the lot.

"Sick shove-it," Ryan shouted, grabbing a forty from his bag, getting back on his board.

Justine pulled a compact from her purse, studied her face from several angles, then snapped it shut. "We're bored."

"Mobb Deep's on tonight at the Bowery Ballroom," Ryan said, rolling past.

Justine made a face.

"Again?" Chris droned.

*

The Kings Park Psychiatric Center entrance was papered with No Trespassing signs and condemnation notices. Justine shoved one foot, then the other, into open chain links, climbing a fence threaded with thick green ivy. She swung a long leg over the top, landing lightly on the other side. Chris and Ryan hopped over after her. I got on tiptoe to hand Ryan his open Olde E—my fingertip brushed against one of his rough knuckles—before struggling over after them, dropping down into knee-high weeds.

Low hills rolled out in three directions—dotted with dense copses of rippling pin oaks and dozens of big brick buildings turning purple in the evening light—stretching all the way down to the Long Island Sound.

Ryan took a swig from his forty and lit another joint. "Five hundred acres," he said, pointing at one building, then another: "Power plant, fire department, bowling alley." Bowling alley? "Pasture over there for livestock." He indicated a field. "Mass grave."

We walked along a gravel path to the closest building: four-story, white-trimmed, red-brick. The windows were all boarded up. It looked like a dead school.

"At its height, the Kings Park Psychiatric Center boarded over ten thousand patients," Ryan continued, again going sort of monotone. "It operated from 1885 until 1996, when the state of New York closed the facility, either releasing or transferring its few remaining patients to the still-operational Pilgrim Psychiatric Center"—it was like he was reading from an encyclopedia—"ending Kings Park's 111-year legacy."

Justine took my hand and threaded our fingers together. I smiled sideways, feeling a weird, tense pleasure, my attention stretched taut between Ryan and Justine like a jump rope being pulled from either side.

Chris removed a camcorder from his backpack and flicked on the light. Ryan kicked the big front door, it swung open, he walked in. The entry was full of suitcases, boxes, and bags, piled high. It smelled like basement. Rotting periodicals were stacked along the water-stained walls. Chris filmed himself rearranging his hair in a broken mirror on the floor. Ryan opened a leather chest, pulled out a white nightgown, lassoed and launched it into the air, silk shimmering down a long hall like a molten ghost. I pictured Justine in the nightgown, curled up on the bed in her white room. I followed them all down the hall, steel-screened windows on the one side, door after door on the other. Paint peeled from the walls, coming off in little parallelograms. The floor had delaminated in places.

Chris ducked into one of the rooms and sat behind a big square wood desk. "How long have you been having these dreams?"

Justine stretched out on her side along a ripped-up leather lounger, one hand propping her head, the other on her hip, like for leg lifts. "Ever since the electroshock, doctor."

The hall opened into a huge, high-ceilinged patient dorm with tall barred windows, everything covered in graffiti. A blue mattress sagged along a partition. I rested against it and Ryan loomed over me, a hand on either side of my head. It seemed like we stood there for a long time.

"When the psychos fucked in here"—his exhalation was hot on my face and stank of malt liquor—"they had to do it all quiet and slow, out in the open." My body flushed. He was going to kiss me. I wanted him to. I held my breath, closed my eyes.

Justine's heels struck the linoleum. Ryan backed away. Chris was chasing Justine across the dormitory.

"I'll order a lobotomy if you don't take your medication!" he shouted after her.

Justine bounced against the mattress, making me bounce too. "Save me from prefrontal surgery!" She squeezed my shoulders and shook.

Ryan finished his Olde E, threw the empty can across the dorm, and walked off. It hit the floor with a tinny echo. I tightened, attraction and annoyance all twisted together.

The dining room was lined with faded food-group posters: broccoli, 3082; peanuts, 4930; grapes, 3093. I could name all the PLU codes, except for fat, which didn't have one; it was represented by a vague agglomeration of yellow triangles.

In the kitchen: huge silver ovens, big black ranges. There was a toaster on the floor, long black electrical cord trailing after it. Justine stood on an industrial scale. I looked over her shoulder. She weighed 113 pounds with her shoes on. My stomach knotted. That was twelve pounds less than me, and she was probably four inches taller.

*

Outside the air was thick and lukewarm. The night made everything look like a black-and-white photograph: quaint white-shingled houses—probably once doctors' residences—clustered atop silver hills. There was a half-burnt-down barn in the near distance. Farther off was a tall, curious shape in silhouette: a building climbed like a black staircase into the gray sky. We walked toward it in silence, up and down the grassy inclines. Justine trotted ahead, arms at her sides, hands fanning.

We climbed in through a broken window. The sill was thick with sediment. Chris's camera light swept across a ransacked room: overturned chairs, a three-legged bench. A pool table lay on its side near a bashed-in TV. Ryan kicked over an old sewing machine, and I jumped at the racket, caught at the edge of what turned out to be a Ping-Pong table. Chris stood at the center with the camcorder, spinning in a slow circle. We spun with him, following the spotlight, which revealed a mural, stretch by stretch. The mural wrapped around the entire space, spanning all four walls. It showed a cartoonish version of what the room might have looked like at one time: two men in light-blue button-down shirts playing chess; two others in white jumpsuits holding little paddles around that very same Ping-Pong table. The figures were weirdly proportioned, warped, out of balance. The chess players looked like they were melting into the board; the tiled floor seemed to lurch, the Ping-Pong players losing their footing, about to fall over.

Justine

Chris spotlit a bald man sitting in a corner wearing a strait-jacket, purple rings around his eyes. Next to him, the only woman depicted sat erect in a white dress, hands folded in her lap, but I couldn't see her face; the wall crumbled at her neck, disfiguring everything above the shoulders.

"My grandmother painted this mural," Justine whispered. "She was a patient here. She died here." I wasn't sure whether to believe her.

*

Outside it was almost totally dark, and the buildings and trees: everything looked menacing. Chris and Ryan walked ahead, and Justine leaned on me.

"Walking in grass this tall, that's how it feels to drink on medication." She wobbled. "It's like moving through Jell-O."

The upward-lifting *O* in "Jell-O" seemed to expand, becoming almost visible, creating an opening, a circle around us, some kind of intimate space. I felt it but didn't know what to do with it. I should've said something. Asked something? I squeezed her little wrist, watching the boys' backs, making sure they didn't get too far ahead. What medication?

"It's the new shoes," I said, too fast, just to say something. It wasn't the right thing though.

"Help!" She clutched at me and laughed, tripping over old railroad tracks.

"Train used to stop here." Ryan looked back at us. "The ward had its own Long Island Rail Road station."

"Yeah?" I asked. The *O* closed. Justine released my arm. I felt guilty but also relieved.

We entered a low single-story building. From the outside it looked municipal. There was a kind of reception area, a short hall, and then a cement-floored room with a wheeled silver table in the middle and big drawers built into the wall. Ryan grabbed a scalpel and threw it at the door; it stuck like a dart. Justine wandered over to the drawers. She pulled at a knee-level handle. The drawer slid open, and she climbed onto a long metal tray. She lay down, folded her arms across her chest, and closed her eyes.

"Push me in!" she shouted.

"Do it," Chris said, recording.

I pushed. She disappeared into the wall feetfirst. Her voice was muffled; she sang something about a comatose girlfriend.

Ryan threw what were probably autopsy tools at the drawer: what looked like Grandma's hacksaw, scissors, cartwheeled through the air, clanged against the metal, and clattered to the ground. Chris shook his head behind the camera.

"La la la la," Justine sang over the metal clangs, "la la la la la."

I couldn't stand it. I pulled out the tray and she jumped up, stretching her arms over her head as though energized after a nap.

We walked back toward the car. Justine skipped. Two flashlights flared from the street side of the fence. There was a cop car parked right behind mine, but no one turned to run. They kept walking. Ryan put his hand on the small of my back, half like he was reassuring me, half like he was just pushing. He climbed back over the fence like nothing, approaching the cops on the other side.

"Damn," the Black cop said. "It's the lieutenant's kid."

Ryan waved.

"Shit." The white cop spit on the side of the road. "Go home and give your mother a kiss."

"Give your little sister a kiss!" The Black one laughed.

I unlocked Grandma's Escort and we all got in.

"Fuck off, Sarge," Ryan shouted, pulling the door shut. He winked at me in the rearview.

*

The next day at work was slow, and boring without Justine. I worked with Michelle. She held a plastic bag full of peanuts in her plump fist.

"4930?" I tried.

53

"These are salted," she sighed, blowing those thin bangs back from her narrow forehead. "4932." Michelle had the hair of a baby chick. She punched the code into the register and slid the bag down to me. It joined the other items at the foot of the checkout: regular Coke, nacho cheese Doritos. I eyed the woman who presumably ingested these things. I unfolded one paper bag, slid a second inside, and punched it open, but the second didn't unfold entirely, I couldn't get it to align with the first; I was furious. Michelle passed a tub of Breyers Neapolitan ice cream over the sensor. I fit it at the bottom of the double paper bag with a carton of milk and stacked a tub of sour cream and a bar of cheddar on top, just like Justine taught me. I loaded the bags into the cart, bent forward, reached my hands to my feet.

"Back hurt?" Michelle asked.

I nodded, grasping the counter edge as blood rushed from my head. A field of white stars opened up, then closed again. I was starving.

"Just wait and see what it feels like in three years."

I stared at the candy rack and felt those twelve excess pounds—that was more than Marlena weighed—at my hips, in my thighs. Michelle bent over the conveyor belt and scratched a lottery ticket with a nickel.

"I won!" she shouted.

"You what?"

"Two dollars."

"It's freezing in here."

"Not really." Michelle offered me a sweatshirt so hideous I preferred to stay cold. "Quick break?" She checked her Tamagotchi. "Mimitchi turned into a teen!" She switched off the lane light. "If Theresa asks, I'm reshelving."

I looked at the new *Vogue*. Nicole Kidman descended a spiral staircase in a gray silk sleeveless gown, hair piled on top of her head, a choker encircling her neck like a diamond vine. There was something so delicate, precious, and ultimately cold about her arched eyebrows, her little nose, her serious gaze, her entire way of being that annoyed me. I put Justine there with her on the stairs and they passed each other wordlessly, without even the slightest acknowledgment, exiting opposite sides of the magazine cover like rivals in a historical period drama.

A hand hit the conveyor belt hard, unsettling the magazine. Blood-red nails, a gold charm bracelet dangling from a slim wrist. I followed a tan arm up to a shoulder, a tense neck tendon, idling for a moment at an impeccably formed ear, lovely little lobe sparkling with a big diamond stud. Gorgeous girl.

"Were you at the psych ward last night?" Her voice was raspy and tight.

I closed the magazine, rested my hands on the cover.

She looked me up and down, lips pursed, brow hard, big dark eyes flashing. "What, this one doesn't talk?" She was short, and not thin—plump, even—and radiant, hair shining too, slicked back into a low tight bun.

I didn't know what to say. I didn't even know who she was. But I knew then that Ryan was hers. Had he told her about me, or had it been Justine?

"You think you're the first one?"

I pressed my lips together. There had been no kiss, only a hand at the back.

She laughed, shaking her perfectly round head like I'd said it out loud. "You know what?"

I held my breath.

She just smiled and walked out, twirling a key chain around her finger, a big yellow Northport Yacht Club floating fob, a BMW logo. She was probably wearing real Chanel Vamp nail polish, not knockoff Revlon Vixen. I didn't breathe until she was out of sight.

When Michelle got back, she checked her Tamagotchi again. "It almost died!" she groaned. "You have to tell me if it beeps when I'm away from the register!"

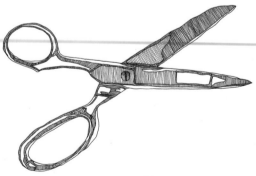

FIVE

I inhaled Marlena's downy little furs, suspended in space, lit up by the morning sun.

"How lazy you are," I said, burying my face in her side. "*Din latta misse*," I hissed.

She lifted a paw in warning, then gnawed at a claw. The way the light came through the window, her face was half lit, half in shadow, one pupil huge and the other just a narrow black slice. Her tiny rib cage winged in and out with each quick breath.

I heard if you blink your eyes really slowly and deliberately, it mimics the way a cat communicates contentment. So I thought, eyes open: "I"; eyes closed: "love"; and "you," eyes open again.

I got out of bed, used the bathroom, emptying myself, not showering yet since water adds weight to hair. I removed my pajamas and folded them neatly beneath my pillow. I made the bed, then pulled the scale out from under it, tapped it with my toe, waiting for the zero to appear. I stepped onto the center, experiencing a kind of merry anxiety as the green lights formed the digits 124.5.

I found a half-filled composition notebook, located the first blank page, and drew an *x*- and *y*-axis along the bottom and left edges, then marked the *x*-axis with dates and numbered the

y from 115 to 125. I penciled in a small circle at July 1, 124.5.
I wrapped a cloth tape measure around my chest, my waist,
my hips, then noted the measurements: "B 35, W 26, H 36."
I thought of something we'd read in English class and flipped
back through the notebook to find my *Lolita* notes: ". . . thigh
girth (just below the gluteal sulcus) seventeen . . ." I took my
thigh measurement and added it—"T 22"—to the list.

I sat on the shower floor and shaved my legs, pulling a razor
across my inner thigh. Why couldn't you just slice the flesh
off? Wouldn't it just scar over? I skimmed off a thin layer
of skin covering an ingrown hair at my groin, squeezing the
flesh around it, pushing a coarse black bristle to the surface,
watching the blood come, then wash away with hot water. I
pinched at the little pockets of fat inside and above my knees,
at my armpits. I shaved the few hairs off my big toes. My pinkie toes curled under. They looked deformed.

"Didn't you just do that?" I stood barefoot, wrapped in a
towel, looking into the kitchen.

Grandma was on her hands and knees with a sponge and
a bucket. She was playing her Perry
Como *Today* tape. "*Det
är smutsigt igen*," she
said, pulling at her
pants waistband. "Too
tight." She stood up, got
scissors from the drawer,
and cut the elastic. "I hate when

it's tight." She slammed the drawer. "I was up at 4:00 a.m. this morning digging up the damn rhododendron. You want juice?"

"*Nej.*" I shook my head and the towel wrapped around it unraveled, leaving my hair in a wet tangle. "Liquids are a waste of calories."

"*Vad?*" She fished her dentures out of a glass next to the sink, popped them into her mouth, and took the Fancy Feast bag from the cabinet. Marlena shot into the kitchen at the crinkling sound and meowed at her empty bowl. Grandma tried to pour the food, Marlena got in her way, and Grandma kicked her. The cat yowled, then was back at the full bowl again like a magnet.

"This isn't a farm."

"He's so lazy." Grandma waved her hand in dismissal.

"She."

"How beautiful you look today." Grandma smiled, getting back on her knees. She sang along with Como about Hawaii in her deep alto. She seemed to have picked up an affected vibrato, I guessed from church. "There's still pie," she said.

"No."

"How about cookies?" She looked up at me. "I'll make *pepparkakor*. Your mother loved *pepparkakor*."

My stomach got tight. "That's for Christmas." I bit the inside of my lip, it bled.

Grandma wrung the sponge into the bucket. "She doesn't want nothing," she said, vigorously scrubbing. She returned to her singing.

I tiptoed across the wet floor and got the leftmost yogurt from the fridge.

"Don't you love Perry Cuomo?" she asked.

"Mario Cuomo," I said. "Perry Como."

"Well excuse me for living," she said. "The car smells, you know."

*

I left early for work and drove around for a while, trying to empty the gas tank. I went past Justine's street but not her house. I drove past their high school. The sign out front— "Northport High School: We Plan to Succeed"—had been spray-painted over to say "Northport, a High School: We Plan to Smoke Weed." Funny.

I saw Ryan inside the Express Mart and pulled into the Hess station. He sauntered over, hands shoved into the pockets of huge khaki pants belted halfway down his flat ass. As he took the big headphones from his ears, I switched the radio station from Z100 to Hot 97. He nodded at me through the windshield, making that same puckered face of disdain. I pulled cat hair from my shirt. When I rolled down the window, he grinned a little.

"You like Black Star?" He lifted his chin, looking down at me.

"What?"

He pointed at the pump.

"Regular."

"Black Star," he said, squinting at the car stereo. "'Respiration,' featuring Common, from the '98 album *Mos Def & Talib Kweli Are Black Star.*" When he inserted the pump into the tank, I felt a warm embarrassment. He paced back and forth, frowning, hands in his pockets, one of them bulging with his Discman.

"Sure," I lied.

He flashed that smug smile. "Know where they got their name?"

I shook my head, feeling momentarily tender, wanting him to tell me. He just needed to tell someone something.

"The Black Star shipping line, founded in 1919 by Pan-Africanist Marcus Garvey, organizer of the Universal Negro Improvement Association," he said, zoning out on the Dunkin' Donuts across the street. "In fact," he continued, forgetting me, as if off reading a book by himself somewhere, "reggae singer Fred Locks, an adherent of the Rastafari faith, first reintroduced the idea of the Black Star Line to a Jamaican audience with his 1976 hit 'Black Star

Liner,' which has been called one of the most important song in reggae music of the 1970s."

The pump signaled disengagement, breaking his meditation. He looked at me, checking to see if I was still listening. I smiled.

"In 'Black Star Liner,' Locks portrays Garvey as a Moses-like prophet," he said, pleased, I could tell, that I seemed to be listening. For a moment he didn't look ugly. He looked sort of normal. I kind of liked his freckled face.

"Know what?" he asked, suddenly friendly. "What you need is one of my custom-made educational mixtapes. The best in tristate hip-hop from '87 to present. $11.97."

I handed him twelve, fingertips grazing his dry palm.

"Yo!" he shouted, but not at me.

Another boy rolled toward us on a skateboard. He was wearing a wool winter hat even though it was eighty degrees. He hopped off and tucked the board under his arm. "Just an O."

"Word." Ryan pulled a sandwich-size Ziploc stuffed with weed from the windshield wash bucket. "My house," Ryan said to me, "after work." He gave me the address, then turned to watch the other boy count out several twenties.

*

Justine wasn't at the Stop & Shop yet, but Michelle was. She held out two puffy white fists. "Pick a hand."

I tapped the right one. She flipped it, spreading her fingers to reveal a tiny key in her pillowy palm.

"Your very own register key!" She smiled, shaking her left fist next. I obliged, touching her knuckles. In that hand: a yellow, egg-shaped Tamagotchi, just like the one on her key chain. "Congratulations!"

"Thanks."

"You can take aisle four," she said, pressing a button to activate my new digital pet. It beeped. She turned the screen to me. A round little eight-bit creature appeared at the center.

"Is it a cat?"

"It's Mimitchi," she said, like that would mean something to me. "You have to feed it and play with it." She pushed another button. "Otherwise it dies." She handed me the Tamagotchi.

I threaded the little key through the key ring. It made me sad. Three years she'd been working here. "Do we have those pine tree things?"

"What?" She blinked.

"That hang, you know? From the rearview mirror?"

"Freshener." She nodded. She pointed to a rainbow display of them below the windows, above the charcoal. They were beautiful, hanging there in color order.

A woman with a stack of silver bangles swung a six-pack onto the conveyor. Her perfume was musky. Her long, highlighted curls looked crunchy.

"ID?" I asked.

"Ha!" the woman laughed. "You're sweet." Tanned skin creased around her mouth. She handed me her license, bangles jangling. The tips of her nails sparkled with rhinestones.

I saw my biology teacher wheeling a cart down the cereal aisle and took my break a little early so she wouldn't see me. She had a way of looking at me—concerned, like I was about to cry. I sat at the card table in the windowless cinderblock break room. I had developed a special ritual to make meals last as long as possible, first setting the strawberry yogurt at the very center of the table, then peeling off the foil lid. I scooped out the creamy pink substance in the tiniest possible spoonfuls, wrapping my mouth around the utensil and sucking the velvety stuff from the hard metal, anticipating and even savoring that strange aspartame aftertaste.

Theresa came in and put a Tupperware in the microwave, the drone and beep interrupting my vigil. She sat down opposite me with leftover lasagna. I didn't see any gray at the roots of her dark middle part. I scraped every last trace of yogurt from inside the plastic container.

"That's your lunch?" she asked, wiping the side of her mouth, orange oil marking the paper towel. She smelled like hair spray. She was practically phosphorescent, her skin like a mirror. Her eyeliner was immaculate.

I licked the cakier stuff from inside the lid.

"Honey," she said, and I tightened. "Have you ever considered electrolysis?"

"What?" I stuffed the foil into the cup.

"I mean like for this." She ran her finger along her upper lip.

I touched my face. "I bleach that."

"Well, just so you know," she said, sliding a business card across the table. "I'm not just the manager here. I'm also an aesthetician. I do electrolysis out of my house two days a week."

That's why her face was like that. The mozzarella on her lasagna was starting to harden.

*

The afternoon was slow. I wondered where Justine was. I skimmed an article about Michael Kors in *Vogue*. They said Kors was born "in Long Island," but you don't say "in Long Island," you say "on Long Island." "On." At the next register, Michelle read *People*.

"Listen to this," she said. "Earlier this month, rap star Puff Daddy walked free at the end of the trial which could have seen him face up to fifteen years in prison. Combs said the trial forced him to reevaluate his life, as well as drop his Puff Daddy alias. He now wants to be known as"—she started laughing—"P. Diddy."

"What?"

Justine didn't come in until the very end of our shift. Her eyes were red. I wondered what was wrong with her. She looked at the magazine over my shoulder. A girl in a white bikini leapt across the beach, a red-and-blue-striped towel flying like a cape behind her, cheeks flushed, eyes shining, long blonde hair whipping in the salty sea breeze, her skin radiating a healthy matte gleam.

"Carmen Kass." Justine nodded at the photo. "She just got a DWI. Her BAC was triple the limit."

"I don't need a ride home today," I said.

She shrugged.

*

I drove to Ryan's. Garfield Place was all small Cape Cods and compact ranches, with patchy backyards, old barbecues, and aboveground pools. I pulled up to 61: a pea-colored, white-shuttered Cape. I hung the pine tree–shaped air freshener from the rearview mirror. For a second I felt like I wasn't going in. But then I wondered which window was his.

"Hello, may I help you?" A serious little girl answered the door in pajamas a few sizes too small. I followed her tangled red head through the living room, which was dim and crowded with a mushroom-colored couch and matching chair with a large brown stain on the arm. I pictured Ryan's cop dad dozing, knocking over a beer as he drifted into a foggy slumber.

I trailed the girl into the kitchen, the cabinets a dark wood veneer, the countertops a dull yellow. A window above the sink let in the tiniest bit of light. I stood there and watched her pour a gallon of gin down the drain. It felt like a weird little performance just for me.

"He's upstairs," she said without turning around. I followed the music to Ryan's room. I put my ear to the closed door and listened for a minute. Layers of fuzzy guitar looped in vague figure eights. I knocked.

"Yeah."

I opened the door. The room reeked of weed.

"Shut it behind you." Ryan lay on his bed watching *Real Stories of the Highway Patrol*. His floor was covered with shirts, socks, skateboards. A stack of *Thrasher* magazines spilled from a plastic laundry basket. Loose change was

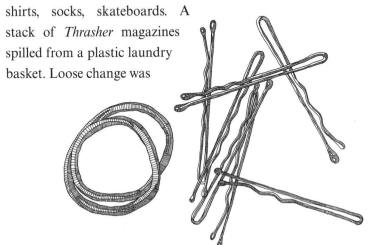

scattered everywhere—pennies, nickels, even quarters—along with crumpled receipts, used-up matchbooks, a couple of lighters, and so many roaches. I saw near my foot what was most likely a girl's black hair elastic, a few bobby pins.

"This episode's dope," he said, gesturing toward the TV. "Calvin Johnson and Doug Martsch talk their way out of getting arrested for possession." He didn't get up from the bed.

"Your sister just dumped a gallon of gin into the kitchen sink."

"Yeah, Eileen hates when Mom drinks," he said. "Hepato-cellular carcinoma."

"What?"

"Liver cancer."

"Oh. Sorry."

"I'd drink too if I was married to the lieutenant."

His walls were lined with CDs and cassettes organized with the precision of a retail display. I studied the spines. They were alphabetized: Black Rob, Black Sheep, Black Star— thousands of albums—Ice Cube, Ice-T, Ill Bill, Illmind. I stumbled over a skateboard and sat down by him on the bed. His pillowcases didn't match his sheets. I felt something under my thigh. It was a book: *Signifying Rappers: Rap and Race in the Urban Present*. I placed it toward the foot of the bed. He flipped through channels. Stephen King got hit by a car?

"Wait," I said. Drew Barrymore walked along a dock with a fat man.

"Don't you know what this is? *The Amy Fisher Story*."

"I think I heard Joey Buttafuoco's a wrestler now?"

"Amy Fisher's a porn star."

"Really?"

He shrugged.

"I came for the tape."

"I have it," he said, then turned off the TV and looked at me. My body felt like it was boiling off. He stood, unbuckled his belt, and dropped his pants to the floor. His boxers were white with maroon stripes. He removed his shirt and his torso was pale, ropy, and all cut up. I mean everywhere: cuts striping the insides of his biceps, some raw, some scabby. I wanted to touch him. Something about the cuts made me realize I'd wanted to touch Ryan all this time. He was a real naked person standing there, all cut up.

I sat forward on the bed and stretched out my hand, but before it could reach him he took my wrist and pushed me down on the bed. The sheets were greasy. He took off my sneakers, my cutoffs—leaving my socks—and lay on top of me. His hair was dirty. I could feel his erection against my thigh, then inside. We looked straight at each other the whole time very seriously, not even blinking. After a while he pulled out and pressed against my pubic bone, coming on my stomach. His heart beat hard against my chest. He breathed heavy onto my neck. His ear touched mine. We lay there for a minute.

Then he slid off me and knelt on the floor. He grabbed behind my knees and pulled my pelvis to his face. He started out licking. I crossed my arms. Then it was more like he was kissing. My arms fell to my sides. I shuddered, closed my eyes, tried to hide my surprise when I came. Ryan looked up and nodded. He picked a sock up off the floor and wiped my stomach. We put our clothes back on. He handed me the cassette tape. I took it, shaky.

"Thanks," I said, hovering at the door.

"Shut it behind you."

I ran out past Eileen. "Bye."

She didn't look up from the TV. She was watching *Jeopardy!*

When I stepped outside, I saw Ryan's mom pulling into the driveway. All I could think was I had sex and she had cancer. She heaved a grocery bag out of the back seat, offering a weak smile. I gave a weak wave.

I slid the tape into the deck and sat in the car for a while, listening, looking up at his window. I had sex with Ryan. There was no condom. He just stuck it in there without even asking. Sex with Ryan was different from sex with Matt. With Matt, sex was less like doing and more like watching, like I was observing other people having sex. The main thing was whether or not it would look good from the outside. Like was it good enough to be in a movie? What was the best facial expression? What percentage of the time did I keep my eyes closed versus open? When Ryan touched me, it was like he just touched me. I felt his actual hands on my actual body. We were real human beings having sex for three minutes. Of course, I'd never tell anyone. Ryan was a dirty, drug-dealing cutter. But I loved every second of it. It might've even been the best thing I'd ever done in my entire life.

There was only one book about Marcus Garvey in the Huntington Public Library: *Black Moses*. It was olive green and wrapped in a shiny clear plastic jacket. Garvey was on the cover in a military uniform, looking very serious, wearing a huge, impossible hat I didn't understand—it looked like bagpipes.

I fell asleep listening to the tape that night.

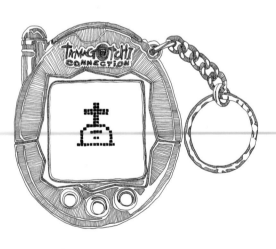

SIX

The Stop & Shop back lot was almost empty. The streetlamps wore halos. My thighs stuck to the hood of Grandma's Escort, it was so humid. Justine inched closer to me, our hips touching, bare legs stretched out side by side. I rested my heels on the front bumper, angling my toes down so my calves looked longer. Justine fiddled with my hair, braiding then unbraiding it in places. Her fingertips brushed my neck. A bead of sweat slipped down my sternum. Airplanes made cane-shaped contrails in the dim sky: takeoffs and landings at Islip, LaGuardia, Newark, JFK.

Chris balanced his camcorder on the hood alongside Justine and me. The boys skated around stray shopping carts, recording tricks on video. Ryan popped the tail of his board, hovered, spun the deck 180 degrees, landed with a slap, rolled back around, did it again. He wasn't graceful like Chris. There was an abrupt, ropy energy to his movements that threatened the unexpected.

After one particularly deft spin, he caught an edge and fell flat on the asphalt. He examined his palms; they were cut. He walked toward me, and I wasn't sure whether it was a hurt knee or just his low-slung pants that made him limp. I hopped down and rooted around the glove compartment. Grandma

81

had Band-Aids. Ryan smirked but laid his hands on the hood. I peeled a bandage from its plastic backing and brought it toward his bloody palm, slow and shaky, like leaning in for a kiss. I thought of the other cuts on his torso.

"Yo!" He brought up the hand like a stop sign. He leaned into the car and edged up the stereo volume. It was the tape he'd made.

"Once again, my friends," he rapped along, "Long Island."

Chris put a hand to his ear and held out the other arm like we were at a luau, rolling his hips to the beat. It was gorgeous.

Ryan gave me his hand back. I held it in mine, dusted off the gravel, and laid down one Band-Aid, then another, pressing the sticky ends into his skin.

"Do you know who this is?" He had a hangnail.

"De La Soul," I said.

"*Stakes Is High* was their first critical triumph in seven years"—he offered me his other hand—"since *3 Feet High and Rising*."

"Critical triumph," Justine mouthed into her mirrored compact.

Chris swung his arms with the music. He went up on alternating toes. He grabbed the brim of his Yankees cap, shifted it forty-five degrees. His shirt rode up, exposing a tan slice of hip. I tried to imagine him and Justine naked. It would be like pressing plastic dolls together.

Ryan raised a finger in the air like he could touch the sound, snaked his head to the bass. "Freeport, Uniondale to Long

Beach," he sang along, "to them girls out in Huntington." He smiled at me. I was surprised he'd even registered that I went to Huntington High School.

"X Games!" Chris shouted. He tossed his skateboard into the trunk.

Ryan and Justine both bolted for shotgun. He beat her there. She slapped his forearm. He pulled the door closed fast, just short of catching her hand in it. We drove to Ryan's house. He gave me directions like I'd never been there before.

"You read that?" He gestured at *Black Moses* on the dash.

"Started it," I lied.

He paged through the book. Justine wrenched it from him, pulling out the envelope I'd stuck inside, my first paycheck. She tore it open like it was addressed to her.

"$116.28." She dusted my cheek with it.

"It should be at least—"

"Taxes."

That much? I pulled into 61 Garfield just before Ryan said "here," and he narrowed his eyes. Eileen was there, cross-legged on the big mushroom-colored easy chair, lit up blue by the TV screen. Chris ruffled her red hair, but she didn't

acknowledge him. We plodded downstairs to the basement, which was furnished with another TV, a pool table, a sooty velour couch, and a mini-fridge. Dusty old soccer trophies lined one of the baseboards.

Ryan switched on the TV, got a beer from the fridge, slumped on the couch, and lit a bong. Chris racked a rainbow of pool balls into a triangle. He leaned across the table for a break shot like a cat about to attack. Justine twirled her cue like a baton and tossed it into the air, dislodging one of the drop ceiling tiles.

"Yo!" Ryan shouted, not taking his eyes off the TV.

I settled down next to him. He tore open a bag of Lay's, took a handful, passed the bag to me. I shook my head. He gave me the bong instead. I took a hit. The water bubbled. I felt myself relax, my shoulders lower, my jaw unclench. My re-flection changed in the TV screen: face lopsided, cheek melting, pulled by the knot of tension in my neck. My mouth sloped down from left to right, a sideways line. I scooped a fistful of potato chips, shoved them into my mouth all at once. They tasted insane. I

felt the fat flood my system: little yellow triangles traveling through my intestines and flowering outward, forming lumpy colonies above my knees. I was so high I was sure Ryan could hear my heart beat.

A person named Tony Hawk kept trying to land a 900, a skateboarding trick no one had ever done before. Chris stopped to watch, using his cue like a cane, weight on one foot like a classical statue. Hawk rode up one side of the half-pipe, then the other, gaining speed before flipping two full airborne somersaults, then losing the board, landing on his knees.

"Stoops!" Ryan shouted, throwing an empty beer can at the screen.

Hawk had ten tries. He attempted the trick again and again, each time failing to land on the board, sliding down the steep half-pipe slope on kneepads. He fell again on the tenth attempt.

"Stoops!" Justine echoed Ryan. The eight ball flew between Ryan and me, not far from my head, narrowly missing the screen.

"Jesus, Justine," Ryan said without turning around.

They gave Hawk one extra chance. That time he landed the trick. Fans crowded around the half-pipe and hoisted him over their heads. We took bong hits.

"I just focus on something and I have to do it," Hawk told the cameras. "I'll either get hurt, taken to the hospital trying it, or I'm gonna make it."

Justine perched on the couch arm beside me. She draped her long arm around my shoulders. "Drive me home, Alison," she whispered into my neck.

"I'm too high."

She ran her hand through my hair, seized a tuft, and yanked it hard. Chris gestured toward the stairs.

"Let's go to Nina's," she said, following him up. "She's having people over." I heard the door shut behind them.

Ryan nodded at me. He took off his pants, boxers, and socks, leaving his T-shirt. I knelt down and did what he wanted. It took a while, my jaw got sore, it tasted like when you chew on a balloon. But it was satisfying to satisfy someone.

He got up, put his boxers back on. I followed him upstairs. Eileen was gone. I thought we'd go to his room, but he opened the front door and motioned me out.

"Night," he said.

I heard the door lock behind me. The lamp across the street flickered. Crickets chirped. A truck drove by. There was a slug in the driveway, thin mucus trail flashing after it. I started the car. Ryan's tape was still playing—a hip-hop version of "I Shot the Sheriff." The light switched on in his window. I drove home.

*

The only thing I really missed about Matt was his warm bulk, just lying next to him, like that thing when I felt his body lurch a little as he went from waking to sleep.

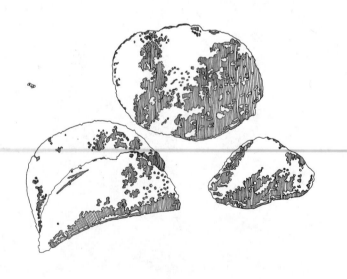

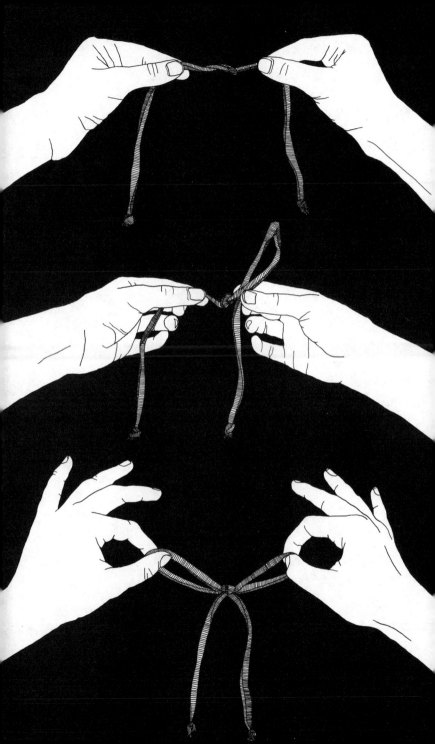

SEVEN

Justine and I lay stomach-down on lounge chairs alongside her pool, sweating in silence. Crows cawed. Bugs floated on the water's surface. Below, a vacuum crept along the vinyl lining. The deck was dilapidated. Grass and dandelions grew from cracks in the asphalt. We drank vodka and Diet Coke. The vinyl chair straps dug into my thighs, making red stripes on my flesh like meat on a grill.

Justine stood up and stretched, bikini top hanging loose across her flat chest, ribs visible, the gap between her thighs impossibly wide. She curled her toes over the pool's edge, swung her arms, shifted to the balls of her feet, and dove in. Justine shot across the water. She floated stomach-up, eyes closed, hair fanning. Her limbs drifted. Justine's body was as smooth and white as a shell's inside, like I could put my ear to her stomach and hear the Atlantic. I wanted to touch her ribs. I wanted to untie the strings at her neck, triangles floating away to reveal the flat nothing they covered. I wanted to be inside her body, drawing her knees and arms up, pushing them down against the water, propelling myself across the pool's glittering surface.

When Justine climbed out, I stood and fell to one knee, drunk. She laughed and yanked me to standing. We leapt across the lawn. A sprinkler zapped at our calves.

Inside, her mother sat with a newspaper at the kitchen table. "You're dripping everywhere," she said, not looking up. Her voice was soft. She sounded far away.

Justine refilled our drinks. Her mother didn't seem to mind that. Her glass was full too. I positioned my legs hip-width apart, trying to make that same space between my thighs.

"Are there calories in alcohol?" I asked.

"No." Justine shook her head, pulling a pint of raspberry sorbet from the freezer.

We sat down with her mother. She'd been beautiful once, with that same wide protruding mouth, like she was wearing a retainer. She was faded now, removed, as though she sat behind a fogged-up window. My thighs spread across the woven seat, covered in goose bumps from the AC. Puddles formed on the tile beneath us. Justine and I ate straight from the container, sharing a single cold spoon. The sorbet was tart.

Upstairs, Justine knelt at the toilet on a nubby beige rug, stuck her fingers down her throat, and vomited without a sound. She held my right hand. My fingers were thick next to hers. Grandma had always said I had a man's hands. Justine took nail clippers from the cabinet and cut down my pointer and middle fingernails, clippings falling to the bathroom floor. I knelt, and she took my hair in her hands. I put my fingers in my mouth and coughed.

"Stick them all the way back."

I did what she said. I gagged and a load of pinkish-brown carbonated stuff came up: raspberry, liquor, cola.

"All of it."

I tried again and vomited a well of browner, more acidic-tasting slime. It coated my hand. I rinsed it off. Justine handed me a bottle of Visine. I blinked the drops from my eyes. We toweled off, put clothes on over our swimsuits.

There was a book on Justine's nightstand. It had a bright aqua cover. A thin girl with platinum hair in a shift dress and big cocktail rings lay flat on her back, daydreaming. The title was *Edie: An American Biography*. Her body stretched out around the spine and, when I flipped the book over, extended across the back cover, her white stick legs tapering into pointy silver flats. I paged through, looking at the pictures: a clipper ship, a mansion, toddlers in sailor suits, cute little drawings of what looked like field mice. Next: the New York City skyline,

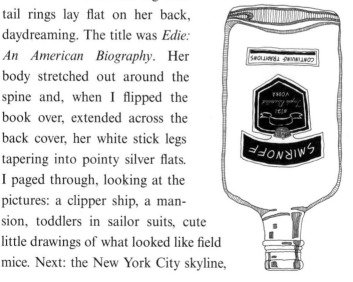

women with big hair dancing at a society ball, Andy Warhol with his arms wrapped around a man called Rod La Rod. And then I saw her in black dance tights arabesquing on a leather rhinoceros, arms spread, cigarette dangling from her hand, metal bracelet circling her tiny bicep, long chandelier earrings dangling down to her shoulders. She appeared to be in a living room: a floral-print divan scattered with pillows, the rhino acting as a makeshift coffee table, a big drawing of a horse on the wall behind her, the kind little girls are always supposed to be making. Her eyes were downcast in concentration, lined dramatically, like a cat.

Justine sat down next to me on the bed. She handed me an eyeliner pen and presented her long face to me, closing her eyes. I leaned in close. She tucked her hair behind her ear. The dull blonde wisps at her hairline looked vulnerable. There was a small colorless mole above her lip I'd never noticed before.

The late afternoon sun came in warm through her bedroom window. Her brow was irritated from tweezing. Her eyelid fluttered. I held my right hand with my left to steady the former, touching the liner to her lid. I felt her breath on my face and I held mine, pulling the felt tip, creating a black arc, the skin of her lid crinkling. I did the winged tip, drawing the line up toward the few light hairs at the end of her brow. I took her chin in my hand and did the other eye, so totally absorbed in the place where her lid met her lash that nothing else existed. I capped the pen. She winked like a baby doll when you shake it. She looked in the mirror, then back at me, smiling. I smiled back.

*

We were going to a Fourth of July party. Heading out, Justine almost fell down the stairs. She grabbed at the banister. At the car, she knocked back the contents of her glass and flung it onto the front lawn. In the car, her hair smelled like grapefruit. I hit a curb and heard a detached hubcap wheeling away after us.

The party was at the end of a peninsula in the richest part of Northport. Old beaters crowded North Creek Road; new cars lined the driveway: Porsche, Mercedes, BMW, Hummer. A red convertible was parked in front of the garage. The license plate holder read: "You call me a bitch like it's a bad thing."

The house was enormous and looked Mediterranean. Floods lit the grounds, trees glowed, an infinity pool stretched out toward the Long Island Sound, gleaming aquamarine. It was the most beautiful pool in the most beautiful backyard of the most beautiful house I'd ever seen.

We got red-and-blue Jell-O shots. They went down sweet, chemical, easy. I held Justine's skinny wrist; she towed me through the crowd. A girl in big sunglasses nursed a Bartles & Jaymes. Her friend used the mirrored lenses to apply lip gloss.

"One in four guys on Long Island's named Mike," I overheard her say, "and half of them are assholes."

Next to them, a boy lay passed out, a Mets cap perched on the most vulnerable stretch of his neck. Two guys in Loyola T-shirts tossed a can of Budweiser between lacrosse sticks. A bad throw and the can rolled down the thick green lawn, which reached all the way to the water, crowded with boats.

Girls stood around laughing, flipping flat-ironed hair. A boy did a keg stand. We hovered at the edge of a group dancing around the lit-up pool. There was one girl who stood out in the crowd, swaying her hips, hoop earrings swinging. I couldn't stop looking at her. She was magnetic, and anyone who denied wanting her was lying. Then I realized I'd seen her before.

"Who's that?" I asked Justine. It was her—the girl who'd come by the Stop & Shop: round face, cupid lip, hard brow.

"That's my friend Nina," Justine said. "This is her party." She nodded at the sprawling villa. "That's her house. You know the pizza place—"

"Nina's?"

Justine nodded. "Her family's."

I loved Nina's Pizza. The slices were just $1.50. They were huge and the crust was thin but flexible enough to fold in half without cracking. Grease pooled into that fold and could be

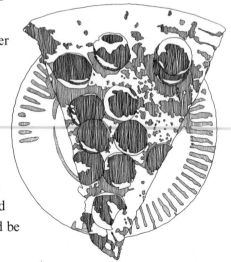

98

poured right off the slice. The
cheese was taut and reas-
suringly rubbery, the
kind that didn't slide or
stretch. It stayed put.
It registered detailed
bite marks.

I smelled weed. Some-
one covered my eyes from
behind. It was Chris—he took
a hit from a joint, then passed it to
Justine, turned on his video camera, and started recording. She
took a hit and held the smoke, wrapped her long hand around
the back of my neck, pulled my face to hers. She pressed her
mouth to mine and blew. Her lips were soft. I wanted to kiss her,
but more, I wanted to be her. I inhaled her exhaled breath, holding her close to me for an extra beat. I grabbed another Jell-O
shot, then went to look for the bathroom, but I was really looking for Ryan.

Nina's living room was like being inside a Louis Vuitton
bag. A religious painting hung above a marble fireplace. Gold
velvet drapes. Kids played quarters on an ornate coffee table.
They looked funny in baggy T-shirts and jeans, slumped on
gold-upholstered sofas. A woman in a halter top leaned over
the table and picked up a shot glass with only her teeth. She
flipped her head, long hair flying, and swallowed the contents
hands-free. The skin at her chest was freckled. A crucifix hung

between her crepey breasts. I figured she was Nina's mother by the roundness of her head, the hardness of her brow. She saw me looking at her and pointed at a door just off the living room. Her fingers were covered in big diamond rings. The bathroom was locked.

"Upstairs," she said, nodding toward an arched doorway that opened up to an octagonal foyer. I climbed the stairs and tried the first door at the top.

"One sec!" someone shouted.

Music came from the end of the hall—a heavy beat. I followed it and stood at the door. It was open just a crack.

I heard Ryan: "You must know this song."

"You must know this song," a girl with a raspy voice mocked him.

"Erik B. and Rakim, 'Paid in Full,' from the '87 album *Paid in Full*, widely considered a touchstone album of golden age hip-hop. Rakim was the first rapper to use internal rhymes, raising the bar for lyricism in the genre and establishing a template for future—"

"Shut the fuck up," the girl rasped, and his lecture was lost to the sounds of fabric rustling, lips interlocking. Shoes hit the floor. The bed creaked under their shifting weight. A sigh. I angled my head but was unable to see them through the narrow crack. I caught only the foot of a canopy bed, floor-to-ceiling windows that opened out to the sound. Something about it felt inevitable, like I'd wanted it to happen. Like I'd almost caused it.

Justine

I tipped the small plastic cup and the Jell-O shot fell to the plush cream-colored rug. A firework cracked. I used the bathroom. The liquid soap smelled like coconut.

*

Outside, everyone stood facing the sound for fireworks. I cut Florida from a cake shaped like the United States, chewed, and spit it into a napkin. I did another Jell-O shot. I saw Chris by the pool. Justine was passed out at his feet with an empty six-pack.

"She's not supposed to drink on the medication," Chris said.

Gold stars filled the sky. The water reflected stippled dahlias and willows. Bursts of light illuminated Justine's face. I wished she could've seen it.

Chris helped me carry Justine to the car, laid her across the back seat, and returned to the party. On the ride back to her house, we didn't speak. Fireworks popped and snapped. We drove past white mansions with black shutters, the Northport Yacht Club, where rich girls had their sweet sixteens and bat mitzvahs. We drove past Northport High School and Nina's Pizza. As we bumped over the railroad tracks, it occurred to me that we lived on the wrong side.

Justine's house was dark. I picked up her empty cocktail glass from the lawn, pulled her out of the back seat, and took her arm around my shoulder. Her eyelids fluttered. The liner had smudged. I walked her upstairs, tried to make her drink water. She took off her dress, dropped it to the floor, and fell onto the bed. She shifted to her side. She drew up her knees and closed her eyes.

I unbuttoned my shirt, slipped off my cutoffs, and lay down beside her. A breeze came in from the open window. I heard the occasional firework. Was she asleep? I turned to my side and tucked my knees, folding into Justine.

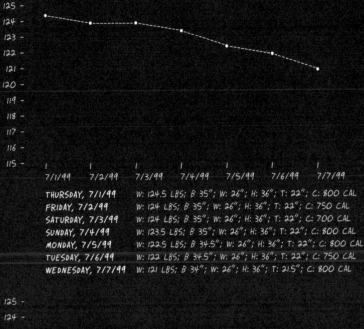

| | 7/1/99 | 7/2/99 | 7/3/99 | 7/4/99 | 7/5/99 | 7/6/99 | 7/7/99 |

THURSDAY, 7/1/99	W: 124.5 LBS; B 35"; W: 26"; H: 36"; T: 22"; C: 800 CAL
FRIDAY, 7/2/99	W: 124 LBS; B 35"; W: 26"; H: 36"; T: 22"; C: 750 CAL
SATURDAY, 7/3/99	W: 124 LBS; B 35"; W: 26"; H: 36"; T: 22"; C: 700 CAL
SUNDAY, 7/4/99	W: 123.5 LBS; B 35"; W: 26"; H: 36"; T: 22"; C: 800 CAL
MONDAY, 7/5/99	W: 122.5 LBS; B 34.5"; W: 26"; H: 36"; T: 22"; C: 800 CAL
TUESDAY, 7/6/99	W: 122 LBS; B 34.5"; W: 26"; H: 36"; T: 22"; C: 750 CAL
WEDNESDAY, 7/7/99	W: 121 LBS; B 34"; W: 26"; H: 36"; T: 21.5"; C: 800 CAL

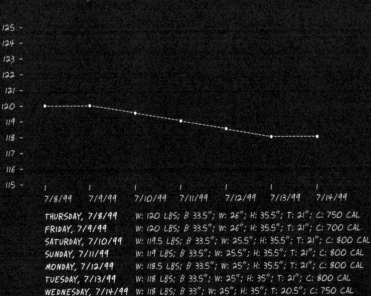

| | 7/8/99 | 7/9/99 | 7/10/99 | 7/11/99 | 7/12/99 | 7/13/99 | 7/14/99 |

THURSDAY, 7/8/99	W: 120 LBS; B 33.5"; W: 26"; H: 35.5"; T: 21"; C: 750 CAL
FRIDAY, 7/9/99	W: 120 LBS; B 33.5"; W: 26"; H: 35.5"; T: 21"; C: 700 CAL
SATURDAY, 7/10/99	W: 119.5 LBS; B 33.5"; W: 25.5"; H: 35.5"; T: 21"; C: 800 CAL
SUNDAY, 7/11/99	W: 119 LBS; B 33.5"; W: 25.5"; H: 35.5"; T: 21"; C: 800 CAL
MONDAY, 7/12/99	W: 118.5 LBS; B 33.5"; W: 25"; H: 35.5"; T: 21"; C: 800 CAL
TUESDAY, 7/13/99	W: 118 LBS; B 33.5"; W: 25"; H: 35"; T: 21"; C: 800 CAL
WEDNESDAY, 7/14/99	W: 118 LBS; B 33"; W: 25"; H: 35"; T: 20.5"; C: 750 CAL

EIGHT

I hadn't eaten all day, and was pleased to see I'd shed a half pound since morning. I penciled in a circle at July 6, 122, and made a line connecting the previous day's dot to the new one. How encouraging it was to see it drawn out on the page like that, a clear descent.

Grandma was at the kitchen table paying bills, 1010 WINS on the radio. I slipped into her bedroom and unwired two of the crystal strands that dangled from the shade of her bedside table lamp. I hooked them into my little hoop earrings for makeshift shoulder dusters. I pulled on a pair of black opaque tights and clasped a silver bracelet around my upper arm. I back-combed my hair high on top and sprayed it in place with Grandma's Aqua Net, fixing the rest into a tight bun at the back of my head. I hunched over a mirror at my desk, making my eyelids black with liquid liner. I couldn't quite get the wings right; they were uneven. I had my mother's eyes, Grandma always said. Marlena leapt onto my lap.

"My tights!" I swatted her to the floor.

She bolted out of the bedroom. I drew in a beauty mark somewhere between Justine's and Edie's, above the lip, to the left. I stood on the bed and held my best arabesque. My body felt light, like I was really high up, balancing on one foot over my whole life.

I sat down across from Grandma with my yogurt. Small sour apples hung from the tree out the window. The radio blared.

"One question," a woman asked, enraged. "How do the administrators explain why they allowed a racist group to exist as an official club with a picture in the yearbook? Wake up and smell the swastikas!"

"*Herren Gud.*" Grandma turned the volume down. She used the cardboard backing of a legal pad and a letter opener to inscribe straight guides across an envelope, then carefully addressed it along the impressions.

"Grandma, Medicaid doesn't care how you address it."

"My writing's no good."

A man with a gravelly voice weighed in. "Police didn't know who was a victim and who was a suspect? Here's a clue: the victims were bleeding and the suspects had guns!"

"Juice?"

I shook my head.

108

She licked the envelope closed. "Today I have to clean the gutters."

She picked up my yogurt. "Work, work, work."

I tapped her veiny hand, smelled the Aspercreme. "I'm not done yet."

"Well excuse me for living."

"There's still some left."

"What do you think John will say under hypnosis today?"

"What?"

"Kate paid Nicole five million to marry Lucas. You think she'll do it?" Oh, *Days*. "Hope is getting fat as a pig."

I heard the pebbles in the driveway. Justine was late; it was after 2:00 p.m. She came in without knocking and plopped down between us at the head of the kitchen table, where Mom used to sit.

"Hi, Grandma," she said.

Grandma?

"*Hej.*"

"Grandma, where are you from?" Justine asked. She picked up Grandma's pen and twirled it between her fingers.

"Sverige," Grandma declared.

"Sweden," I said.

"Stockholm?" Justine asked. She flipped over the Medicaid envelope and started scribbling on it.

"*Nej.*" Grandma shook her head, frowning at the envelope. "The farm."

I hit Justine's hand to make her stop. "Småland," I said.

109

"Like with cows?"

"Of course," Grandma said, smiling. "They named me after the best cow."

"They did not," I said.

"You better believe it!" Grandma said.

"When did you come to this country?" Justine asked.

Grandma took her time answering, as if she were making a complicated calculation. Justine started scribbling again. I took the pen from her. She glared.

"1941," Grandma said, definitively, "on the last boat."

"How do you know it was the last boat?" I asked.

"*Vad*?" Grandma frowned. "Before the war."

"You mean Pearl Harbor?" Justine rested her forearms on the table, long hands outstretched.

"*Ja*," Grandma said, but she didn't know what she was talking about.

"What did you do when you got here?" Justine asked.

"I was a maid," Grandma announced, proud. "For J. C. Penney."

"Like the store?"

"The man."

"Wait, what?" I asked.

"*Naturligtvis*!" Grandma said it like we were arguing. "On Park Avenue."

"You never told me that," I said.

"You never asked."

"What was he like?" Justine interjected.

"Oh!" Grandma hooted. "He was a fresh old man."

"What's that supposed to mean?" I asked.

"It doesn't mean nothing," Grandma replied with a sort of hauteur. "He gave me a recommendation."

*

For some reason I was furious, thinking of Justine sitting there in Mom's spot. On the way to Tower Records, she and I didn't speak. She sang along with Morrissey, going on about being tied to the back of a car. We passed Loehmann's, where I got my junior prom dress.

Chris was already there when we arrived, strolling down the hip-hop aisle. He kept looking up at his reflection in the mirror where the wall met the ceiling. Ryan wasn't there. I meandered around in a way I hoped seemed inconspicuous.

On the news rack, a grid of women looked out from dozens of magazine covers. They asked: "What would you like?" smiling in tight pink sequined or floral dresses, hands on their hips, some of them in motion, this one just bending over to strap on a gold high-heeled sandal on her way out the door. She asked me to keep her company, offering all kinds of useful information on the way to the party: the secret to looking leaner naked, where to buy those gold sandals. She whispered into my ear the names of various pubic hairstyles: landing strip, Bermuda triangle, heart, arrow, postage stamp. I turned my head into the nape of her neck ever so slightly to better smell her perfume.

There was another rack at the back of Tower Records stocked with magazines featuring even more women wearing even less. They also asked: "What would you like?" but their solicitations weren't for me.

I made my face blank, browsing the hip-hop racks, looking for the albums Ryan liked best. I slipped *Stakes Is High* into my messenger bag, peeled off the anti-theft sticker, reapplied it to *3 Feet High and Rising*. I repeated this series of actions with EPMD's *Strictly Business* and Public Enemy's *Muse Sick-n-Hour Mess Age*.

There was a girl standing in the rock aisle who looked like a wonderfully relaxed cat with wide-set narrow eyes, a smattering of freckles across her flat nose, the corners of her mouth turned up at the sides in a sleepy half smile. She pushed her long silky hair away from her face with a languor that made me ashamed of my restlessness. I browsed alongside her, making sure Justine wasn't looking before jamming my bag with a handful of Smiths CDs. Justine was moving toward the exit. As she went out, a cute little girl came in with a heart-shaped face and a dimpled chin, shoulder-length dirty-blonde hair that looked soft to the touch and like it tangled easily.

I saw Fiona Apple's *Tidal* and grabbed it on my way out. I passed close by the girl with the dimpled chin. A diamond Star of David sparkled at her bony collarbone. Her neat little features strained at something behind me.

"Miss." It was a woman's voice.

Justine

My heart hammered. I sped up and didn't look back. I pushed the door open.

"Miss." The woman caught hold of the door. I stopped, watching Justine trot through the parking lot. She got into her car, started the ignition, and drove away. She left me.

I turned to face the woman. She was short and plump, with a broad face and close-cropped hair. A wide face wasn't right for hair like that. She looked as scared as I felt.

Another employee had caught Chris a few aisles behind me. They took us back to the break room. We emptied our bags. They photocopied our licenses and pinned the printouts to a corkboard. I felt nauseous. We waited for the cops in metal folding chairs. Chris took out a copy of *On the Road* and paged through it as though he were simply relaxing at home. The woman flipped through a three-ring binder. She laid it on the table, open to a blurry black-and-white printout of Justine's long face. She set a pen and a piece of loose-leaf next to it.

"We've seen her here before," the woman said.

Chris kept his eyes on the book, turned a page.

I wrote down Justine's name and number.

Chris looked up from his book, straight ahead, not at me. He tilted his head ever so slightly, fluttered his long black eyelashes.

*

The cops led us out through the store. People turned to watch. They put Chris and me in the back of a real police car and we

sat as far apart as we could, looking out opposite windows: Bagel Boss, Bridal Elegance, Cancos Tile. We passed over the Long Island Expressway, rush hour commuters stuck in gridlock below, two glittering strands of headlights in one lane, two blinking columns of brake lights in the other. The sky was an oppressive white.

The Suffolk County Police Department was headquartered in a low, wide concrete building, a huge American flag flapping out front. They put us in a cell. They gave us soda and candy from the vending machine. That surprised me. I ate a Twix bar, drank a regular Coke, and asked to use the bathroom. A cop led me through a row of cubicles. Was one of the men seated there Ryan's dad?

The cop stood at the bathroom door while I went. I knelt at the toilet and stuck my pointer and middle fingers down my throat, like Justine showed me. After a few tries I coughed up a liquid cloud of caramel and chocolate. On the way back to the cell I tried to tell from the cop's face whether he'd heard me.

Once the paperwork was processed, we were instructed to call our guardians. There was no way I could call Grandma. I called Dad. He got to the police station two hours later. He laughed with the cops when they released me, but too far out of range for me to hear what about. We climbed into his pickup truck. It was starting to get dark out. He didn't put on his seat belt. He never did.

"So," he said. "I guess it was about, what, '75?" He paused. "'75. Man." He whistled. "I had a date with a girl named . . .

116

Valerie—beautiful, beautiful girl—but I had no car, right?" He looked over at me like we were thick as thieves. "So I took a walk down to Bay Avenue, hot-wired what I needed, and arrived to pick her up in a baby-blue Coupe de Ville." He laughed, then glanced at me again. "Well, you look great," he said.

I shrugged, suddenly embarrassed by the teased hair, the long earrings.

"Did I tell you about the time I was in for a few weeks out in Riverhead?"

"No." Yes.

"We really pulled one over on this guy. What an asshole. He was down to four days left before parole."

I nodded.

"We made copies of his papers, right? Changed the date from four days to four years. Ha!" he laughed. "The CO was in on it. You should've seen the poor kid—he started crying right then and there, this tough guy." Dad shook his head, smiling. We passed the grade school. "Remember when we used to fly kites back there?"

"Yeah."

He turned up the radio: WBAB. It was some man singing—Eric Clapton, Bob Dylan, I didn't know. Dad drummed his hands against the wheel. We drove over the Mill Pond bridge.

"Hey," I said. "Remember when we used to fish here?"

He smiled.

"Remember that time your truck keys fell over the rail into the water?"

He laughed.

"And"—I squinted, trying to remember—"yeah, right, we were walking down to the other end of the bridge, to the pay phone, right?"

"Yep."

"And the keys, they just shot up out of the pond and into the air. And you stuck your hand out just in time and the keys fell right into it!" The memory didn't make sense. "How did that happen?" I asked. "Was it some kind of fountain?"

"No, no," he said. "We just fished them out of the water with a stick."

"Oh."

"So your grandmother doesn't know?" he asked as we turned onto my street.

I shook my head. He stopped out front, not pulling into the driveway.

"Well, give her my best," he said. He squeezed then patted my knee. It felt like an approximation of my knee, the way he touched it.

I watched him drive away, turned, and saw Grandma there behind the lace in the window.

"What did he want?" she asked as I came in.

"Nothing."

"*Jävla fyllehund*," she said, though I was pretty sure he'd been sober for at least a year.

Justine

Marlena wasn't curled up in her usual spot by my pillow. I looked for her on the La-Z-Boy, went out front and called for her. She didn't come, though. I went to bed.

NINE

I woke to Grandma's shouts from down the hall. "*Fan också!*" she exclaimed, then "*Försvinn!*" a few minutes later.

I found her standing fully clothed in the empty bathtub, scrubbing the tile grout with a toothbrush. Yellow light tunneled in from the window above the toilet. The ammonia smell was overwhelming. I crossed my arms, leaned against the doorframe.

"It's not even dirty," I said.

"*Det är äckligt.*" She shook her head. "Stubborn as a mule, too." Her hair was wet with sweat.

I flipped on the ventilation fan. "Where's the cat?"

"*Vad?*"

"Where is Marlena?" I said, overenunciating each syllable.

"How should I know where he goes?" She ran the toothbrush under the faucet before attacking the moldy grout again.

"She."

"She, she."

Maybe she'd gotten stuck in the garage rafters again. I went to look. There was a piece of folded loose-leaf taped to the screen door. It was labeled "Alison" in Justine's small, neat capital letters. I unfolded it.

"You're a rat whore," the note said.

I crumpled it into my pocket. My eyes got wet. A van passed. The *Daily News* flew out, landing at the foot of the driveway. Our front lawn was covered with pizza, from the apple tree all the way down to the rhododendron.

I got a handful of trash bags and went out barefoot, tiptoed across the pebbles, stepped through the cool wet grass. There were at least two dozen pizzas, maybe three, scattered across the lawn: plain, pepperoni, Buffalo chicken, fra diavolo, baked ziti. A squirrel shot off with a nugget of sausage. Crows picked at a white pie. I could tell by how big they were, and the rubbery cheese, that they were from Nina's. Two had been pulled into the street and ravaged. Raccoons, probably.

I picked up a Sicilian pie by its thick crust and imagined having a bite—I was light-headed—before dropping it into a trash bag. I rushed through the cleanup, shoveling one pie after another into the bags, hoping to finish before Grandma saw. I hoisted the heavy sacks into the garbage cans at the curb. My fingers were oily with sauce. Wet cut grass stuck to my feet. Across the street, Vinny came out in only a robe, shuffling down his driveway. His breathing was labored. He'd had a heart attack a few months back. And just before that his wife had died, hadn't she? Diabetes, I thought. I half waved.

"I'm so sorry, honey," he said, barely able to bend over for his paper. I should have gotten it for him. "I just—" He had a few envelopes in his hand. "I didn't see her, you know?" He made his way to his mailbox, sliding the envelopes inside,

putting up the red flag. "I don't know how she got there."
He rested his hand on the head of his little statue of a man
holding a lantern. "I was backing out here." He pointed at
his driveway. "And I looked. I looked." He shrugged and
slumped. "She was right under my tire." He shook his head.
"I didn't see her," he repeated.

I secured the trash can lid, picked up our paper. His sprinkler hissed.

"Her legs, you know. They were—" He twirled his hand at
the wrist. "Crushed."

Crushed. I nodded. Those little legs. I felt dizzy. I needed
a yogurt.

"Your grandmother was right to put her under," Vinny muttered, padding back toward his house, out of breath
now, robe sash swinging.

"There was nothing
else to be done," he
said, mostly to him-
self, as he went inside.

I washed my hands
at the kitchen sink.
Marlena's food and wa-
ter bowls weren't on the
floor anymore. Her Fancy
Feast wasn't in the cabi-
net. Grandma had already
thrown it out.

ALISON

The line connecting July 6 to July 7 was flat at 120 pounds. My right thigh measured twenty-one inches in circumference. I stripped and stood in front of the mirror screwed to the inside of my closet door. I pulled back the fat between my thighs. I released it and they shuddered. My pubic hair was bushy. I trimmed it with tiny scissors, then weighed myself again, but it didn't make any difference, not even an ounce. I vacuumed the little hairs up with the Dustbuster.

I ate a yogurt in my room and did three sets of ten leg lifts on the bed. Marlena's fur was matted on the fitted sheet next to my pillow. I always had to try to keep her from eating it. She was so small when we got her. I guess I was small then too.

*

I went out and drove around—past the Stop & Shop, past the Hess station, past Ryan's house and Justine's, the LeSabre there in the driveway. I drove past Nina's Pizza and her family's tall front gate and high square hedge, air heavy with the stink of low tide. I drove down Matt's street: half modest two-bedrooms, half with second-story extensions that loomed over the road. Matt's was one of the latter, the new front porch and balcony above it supported by fat white pillars. He was home, his F-150 out front, "Matthew & Son" on the door in big green letters. I went to the Walt Whitman Mall and wandered around Bloomingdale's, spritzed each wrist and either side of my neck with Polo Sport, Happy, CK One, Obsession.

At home, Grandma stood over the stove, dropping pink turkey patties onto a hot frying pan with a slap.

"John and Gina made love in the submarine today," she said, sliding a spatula under a patty. "So John stabbed Stefano." She flipped it; oil splattered. "And Stefano threw him overboard!" She laughed. "You should've seen it." The off-white cooked color crept up the patty sides, out of which oozed gray slime.

I slumped into the La-Z-Boy with a copy of *Vogue*. Milla Jovovich curled her fingers like talons around a bottle of Dior's Hypnotic Poison. Maggie Rizer bounced across the page with pigtails and pom-poms for Clinique. Amber Valletta gazed up lazily from a sun-drenched daybed, light splashed across her chin, cheekbone, brow. JFK Jr. and Carolyn Bessette held hands at a black tie gala. Three women in full-length fur coats trudged across an arctic landscape, long blue shadows stretched across the snow. A satiny robin's egg Louis Vuitton stiletto ground into the center of a splayed white hand.

Grandma set two plates on the coffee table and turned on Fox News. A series of red, blue, and purple concentric circles floated across the continent.

"Large-scale search and rescue operations are taking place across Oklahoma City as the casualty count climbs to thirty-six fatalities and 583 injuries," the newscaster announced.

"Look at that hair," Grandma said, mouth full of food. "It looks like a chicken scratched in it."

I removed the bun and cut the turkey patty into nine little pieces. I doused my plate with ketchup, speared one piece of turkey with my fork, dipped it, slotted it into my mouth, and chewed it exactly thirty-three times. I felt the sugar and salt enter my bloodstream, rush through my body.

"President Bill Clinton is expected to sign a major disaster declaration, allowing the state to receive federal aid," the newscaster continued.

"There's a letter for you," Grandma said, pushing an envelope along the coffee table with a thick yellow fingernail, past her knitting, the candy dish. She switched on the table lamp.

It was from the Suffolk County Police Department. I took my time, dipping and eating a second piece of turkey before reaching over to pick it up. The oscillating fan rattled. I opened it, careful to keep the contents angled toward me. It was a summons.

I sighed, shoving it into my magazine. "Station fundraiser." I took my plate to the kitchen, tilting the bun and seven remaining turkey pieces into the trash.

"I made vanilla pudding," Grandma called from the couch.

I shut myself into my room for the night. I sat on the floor and tore select pages from *Vogue*. I stood on my bed and taped the one of Amber Valletta to the place where the wall met the ceiling. I lined it up next to a picture of Karen Elson and Stella Tennant leaning against a graffiti-covered brick wall in long silk sleeveless gowns. Just a few more pages and I'd have created a border around my whole little room.

*

Justine

That night I dreamt of biology class. Justine was at my lab table, pulling at the ends of her black bob, shoving her hair into her mouth. I sat down next to her. She smiled at a spot slightly to the left of me. The sinews stuck out of her neck.

The teacher circulated through the classroom, placing graded test papers facedown in front of us. She adjusted her glasses and nodded at Justine and me as we both flipped our papers to reveal the letter *A*. I felt the sticky tap of Justine's patent leather Mary Jane against my shoe. Warmth surged up my leg to my groin.

"You all know what today is." The teacher smiled, sitting on her desk and swinging her legs. Her calves bulged in suntan nylons, her swollen feet ballooned from her low block pumps. She had a thickness that I could never tolerate in myself but that I found reassuring in her—a solidity, like Grandma had before she got so old.

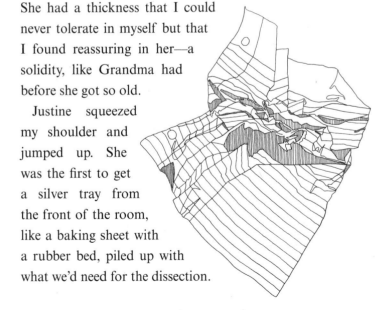

Justine squeezed my shoulder and jumped up. She was the first to get a silver tray from the front of the room, like a baking sheet with a rubber bed, piled up with what we'd need for the dissection.

She moved with a wiry efficiency, short hair swinging at her chin, lining up the scalpel and tweezers, counting the dissection pins with the seriousness of a surgeon.

I got safety equipment from the back of the room. Justine craned her long neck, and I lowered an apron over her head. She strapped on goggles and pulled gloves over her long hands, snapping the latex at her wrists. Her black hair bulged above the goggles strap. She picked up the scalpel and sliced open the plastic, dumping the scrawny cat onto the rubber. It landed with a light thud, stomach up, arms, legs, and tail outstretched. Fluid leaked from the plastic, drizzling onto the tray and over the cat, which was matted, flattened, and smelled fermented.

Justine swatted my arm with the back of her latex-covered hand. She grabbed the tweezers and pretended to pluck her eyebrows, eyes flashing behind the glare of her goggles.

"We'll start by examining inside the oral cavity." The teacher looked on, narrowing one eye and pressing her lips together. "Use your scalpel to cut the membrane that connects the hinges of the cat's mouth and open it wide to examine the inside."

Justine sliced open the cat's mouth and tore the jaws apart.

"You should be able to see and label the esophagus," the teacher continued, "which connects to the stomach, and the glottis, which connects to the lungs."

Justine took hold of the cat's tongue. It stretched at least three inches.

I labeled "tongue" on the lab report diagram, disgusted.

"We'll use a basic X cut to open the specimen's abdomen." The teacher drew an X on the chalkboard. "Make one slice across each leg and connect them with a single cut up the girdle."

Justine made the incisions, used the tweezers to lift the abdominal muscles. She peeled back the skin, affixed it to the rubber bed with the dissection pins. I labeled the lab report diagram: esophagus, glottis, stomach, lungs.

Late afternoon light came in through the half-drawn venetian blinds, striping Justine's face, her long arms and fingers, wrapped around the stainless steel scalpel. The school day was almost over. She sliced the spiderweb-like peritoneum membrane. I wrote our names next to each other across the top of the lab report. She watched out of the corner of her eye, smiling slightly, and pulled the membrane loose. Horrible bright yellow tubes fell from the cat's abdominal walls like little fish-tank plants.

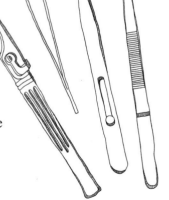

"Those are the fat bodies," the teacher said. "You'll need to remove them to see the other organ systems."

*

Justine wasn't at work the next day. I was relieved. I took a copy of *Seventeen* from the magazine display. Katie Holmes was on the cover. She always wore that same half smile. Michelle appeared at my register, eyes puffy, tears running down her face, making the blonde baby hairs at her ears moist. She laid a copy of the *Daily News* on the conveyor belt, open to the local news.

"Northport Girl Dies in Swimming Pool," the headline read. Next to it: Justine's yearbook picture, her black bob carefully curled under, her wide mouth curled up at the sides, but not in what I'd call a smile. You couldn't really make out her mole. I leaned in close to the newsprint, studied the arrangement of tiny black dots, read the first few lines: "A local teenage girl dove to her death in a tragic accident, breaking her cervical spine in the shallow end of her family swimming pool."

Michelle threw her arms around me, wet cheek at my cheek, fleshy biceps hung over my shoulder bones. Should I have been crying? I felt separate from her, like the space created by the weight I'd lost was a buffer. She couldn't touch me through it.

A woman wheeled up a full shopping cart. I passed each product over the sensor with painstaking precision, the resultant beeps creating a comforting rhythm: Perdue boneless skinless chicken breasts; potatoes, russet, 4072; Tropicana Pure Premium 100% orange juice, lots of pulp. I constructed double paper bags, sorting the refrigerated items in one, frozen items in another. I bagged the produce in layers: first

132

potatoes, then apples, carrots, lemons, lettuce. I experienced especial satisfaction when three large cereal boxes—Lucky Charms, Cheerios, Frosted Flakes—slid snugly into a single bag. I placed each bill faceup into its respective slot in the cash register. I Windexed the conveyor belt at regular intervals.

At noon, I surveyed the cool dairy aisle for my lunch. I did not see any Dannon Light fat-free strawberry yogurt. I stood there long enough—staring at the place where it should've been, between the peach and vanilla—that I got cold. A stock boy I'd never seen before pushed a dolly stacked with boxes of Smucker's Concord grape jelly.

"Dannon Light fat-free strawberry yogurt?"

He stopped and scanned the shelf. "There's blueberry." He pointed. "Or what about low-fat?"

I shook my head.

"Strawberry Yoplait?"

I ran back to my register and scoured the candy rack: Bubblicious in fat hot-pink balloon letters, Hershey's in official silver capitals, Snickers in reassuring blue italics. I tore open and ate an entire bag of M&M's in under a minute, barely grinding the candy shells between my teeth. I rushed to the bathroom and threw up brown with little flecks of rainbow. I started to cry, dug my fingernails into my palms so I'd stop. Theresa came in as I pumped pink liquid soap from the dispenser. She perched her rhinestone-encrusted sunglasses on her head and pursed her lips in the mirror. She looked older under the fluorescent light. Foundation had collected in the fine lines under her eyes. She dragged a fingertip along the delicate skin, redistributing the makeup. I soaped my right hand with my left, hiding my inflamed knuckles. Her lipstick had bled into little rivulets above her lip. She lined them, coated them with gloss. She zipped her makeup bag closed and smacked her lips together. She glanced at my reflection. I dabbed my eyes with a stiff paper towel.

*

Outside, the early evening light turned the parked cars glittering gold and striped the lot with long purple shadows. An old man struggled to get grocery bags from a cart into his trunk. A woman struggled to get her toddler into a car seat. A girl dropped her keys onto the asphalt, picked them up again.

I drove directly from the Stop & Shop parking lot—taking the speed bumps hard and fast—into the Hess station. I saw Ryan inside the glowing Express Mart. He shuffled out, hands pushed deep into his pockets, long braided leather belt hanging down his thigh.

"You heard?" he asked, looking down at me through the open window. His eyes were dark. He shifted his gaze to the Dunkin' Donuts across the street.

I nodded.

He shook his head, arms crossed, drummed his fingers along his biceps. "See you at the wake, I guess," he said.

I shrugged. I mean, I didn't even know her.

Acknowledgements

Jin Auh, Paul Beatty, Yashwina Canter, Alexander Chee, Diane Chonette, Masie Cochran, Shelly Cohen, Aurélien Couput, Elizabeth DeMeo, Melissa Febos, Jessica Friedman, Javi Fuentes, Inger Gibb, Anna Godbersen, Emily Gould, Lauren Grodstein, Thomas Harmon, Ann Harmon Mayes, Ed Henrich, Hermione Hoby, Ajla Hodzic, Pamela Hint, Becky Kraemer, Catherine Lacey, Victor LaValle, Sanaë Lemoine, Nick Maravell, Christiane Manzella, Emma McIntyre, Nanci McCloskey, Monica McClure, Julie Montgomery, Alyssa Ogi, Ed Park, Rob Penner, Craig Popelars, Elizabeth Pratt, Kristen Radtke, Archie Rand, Spencer Ruchti, Kirsten Saracini, Andrew Shurtz, Lori Shurtz, Aaron Smith, Caroline Snyder, Dan Springer, Paul Stephens, Will Stephens, Kiely Sweatt, Molly Templeton, Marie Tennyson, Başak Ulubilgen, Tomas Vu, Mackenzie Watson, Alan Ziegler, Sara Zin